I HEARD THE FRONT DOOR OPEN. IT WOULD BE BETSY COMING TO RELIEVE ME.

It wasn't Betsy. It was Chambrun, accompanied by Jerry Dodd. Chambrun was almost unrecognizable. His face was the color of gray ashes in a fireplace. His mouth was a thin knife slit in his face. His eyes were clouded ice. I guessed there was news of the Willises—bad news. It was worse than that, from Chambrun's point of view. He held out a folded sheet of white paper to me, not speaking.

"Came by special messenger," Jerry Dodd said.

There was one sentence typewritten on the piece of paper. "IF YOU WANT TO SEE YOUR MISS RUYSDALE ALIVE AGAIN TURN THE BOY LOOSE."

———————— ★ ————————

"Readers won't be disappointed . . . fans will love it."

—*Publishers Weekly*

Nightmare Time

HUGH PENTECOST
Nightmare Time

WORLDWIDE.

TORONTO • NEW YORK • LONDON • PARIS
AMSTERDAM • STOCKHOLM • HAMBURG
ATHENS • MILAN • TOKYO • SYDNEY

NIGHTMARE TIME

A Worldwide Mystery/June 1988

First published by Dodd, Mead & Company, Inc.

ISBN 0-373-26001-6

Printed in U.S.A.

PART ONE

ONE

IT WAS ABOUT one o'clock on a summer morning as I walked through the lobby of the Hotel Beaumont, New York's top luxury hotel. The hotel was very much alive at that time in the morning. A debutante function was taking place in the Grand Ballroom, the Blue Lagoon, the hotel's popular nightclub, was going full blast, and the two main bars, the Trapeze and the Spartan, were crowded with customers. I was headed for my office on the second floor when I saw Mr. Cardoza, the maitre d' of the Blue Lagoon, signaling to me. I went over to join him.

Mr. Cardoza looks more like a Spanish nobleman than a headwaiter.

"I've got one that calls for The Man," he said.

The Man is an in-shop name for Pierre Chambrun, the hotel's famous manager. Chambrun is the king, the Mayor, of a small city within a city. Under the Beaumont's roof are bars and restaurants, shops including a pharmacy, a health club, a hospital, a police force, almost anything you could think of asking for in a home away from home. Chambrun knows every inch of it, every small detail of every function. He is a walking computer on the subject of the Beaumont. He also has a personal life which is kept that way—personal.

I am Mark Haskell, head of public relations for the hotel, and one of three people who know where to find The Man in his most private moments. The others are Jerry Dodd, the wiry little former FBI agent who is head of the hotel's security, and Betsy Ruysdale, The Man's storybook secretary who is rumored to *be* his private life.

"What's cooking?" I asked Cardoza.

"I am being faced down by a ten- or twelve-year-old boy," Cardoza said.

"That'll be the day!"

"His name is Guy Willis," Cardoza said. "He and his parents, Major and Mrs. Hamilton Willis, are registered in suite 17C. The boy claims his parents left him alone about nine o'clock, headed for the Lagoon. They planned to be gone for about an hour. They never came back."

"Which shows what a sensational host you are, Cardoza."

"The Major and his lady never came to the Lagoon," Cardoza said. "The boy called down for them, and when I told him they weren't here he came down to see for himself. He insists on seeing The Man. He says his father told him that if he was ever in trouble while staying here, he should go to The Man. No one else will do. Suddenly there's a priest in the act, a Father Callahan, who offers to take the boy under his wing. The boy says he doesn't know him. The priest says he's an old friend of the boy's father. The boy won't budge unless The Man tells him to budge. I know you can reach Chambrun, Mark. Would you mind?"

When Chambrun goes private, nothing short of a bomb threat to his precious hotel justifies his being disturbed. But there was something special about Major Hamilton Willis. Every morning at nine o'clock Betsy Ruysdale and I join Chambrun in his office when he is having his second cup of breakfast coffee. We look over the registration cards of people who have checked in since the day before. Those cards, eventually marked with letters, tell us all there is to know about a guest—his credit standing, whether he's an alcoholic, a husband cheating on his wife, or a wife cheating on her husband. Then there are the initials P. C., which indicate that Chambrun knows something about the guest that is not to be general knowledge. A couple of days ago the Willises' card came to my attention.

"Red-carpet treatment for these people," Chambrun said. "It just may be I owe Ham Willis my life."

The story had made the front pages of the newspapers a couple of years back. Chambrun, who had left the hotel to discuss some financial matters at his bank, was returning when he was jumped, just outside the hotel, by three thugs. They turned out to be Arab terrorists who planned to hold The Man hostage to get some leader of theirs freed from jail. Luckily Major Hamilton Willis turned up at the critical moment, drew a gun, shot one of the terrorists, and held the other two at bay until the police took over.

"It was a near thing," Chambrun said. "I owe him, beyond the ability to pay."

This, I thought, could be the moment. At least he wouldn't resent my breaking in on his privacy. I called a number I had, and Chambrun thanked me.

"Stand by the boy till I get there, Mark. Fifteen minutes..."

I walked into the Blue Lagoon with Cardoza. I saw the boy instantly. He was blond, handsome, wearing gray slacks and a navy blue blazer with brass buttons. I saw at once that he was tense, fighting hard not to show that he was scared. He was at a corner table, his chair backed up against the far wall, staying as far away as he could from the priest, easily recognized by his turnaround collar, who was leaning across the table, talking earnestly. No one else in the Lagoon was paying any attention to him because Duke Hines was on stage, supplying the guests with some of his marvelous jazz-piano music.

Cardoza and I headed for the table. The boy's bright blue eyes widened as he saw us approaching. We were the marines, I thought.

"Guy, this is Mark Haskell," Cardoza said to the boy. "He's talked to Mr. Chambrun, and he's on his way."

The boy stood up, gripping the back of his chair. "Thank you, sir," he said to me.

The priest had also risen. "I am Father Paul Callahan," he said to me. "I'm an old friend of the boy's father. I want to help him if I can."

"I never saw this man before!" the boy said. "He isn't a friend of my dad's."

"How did you know he was in trouble?" I asked the priest. "If you didn't know him by sight—"

"Series of coincidences," the priest said. "A parishioner of mine told me about the fellow who plays the piano here." He gestured toward Duke Hines on the stage. Duke was in the middle of his marvelous version of "Saint Louis Blues." "I found myself in the neighborhood. I grew up on New Orleans jazz, and I thought I'd drop in to hear this man. He's pretty magical."

"About the boy," I said.

"I was just sitting down at this table, shown to it by this head waiter, when Guy rushed up to him. He explained who he was, that his father was supposed to be here, but wasn't. That was the second big coincidence. I was a chaplain in the Air Force ten years ago, Vietnam. Lieutenant Hamilton Willis, now a major, was one of the fliers I knew well. It was almost a miracle that I'd been brought here when his kid was in trouble. I can and will care for him until the Major gets in touch." He moved toward the boy, put an arm around his shoulder. "Come along, son."

The boy wrestled himself free, gave the surprised priest a violent shove, and rushed to me for protection.

"The boy is following his father's instructions," I said. "If he was in any trouble he was to contact Mr. Chambrun."

"I understand that," the priest said. "Of course, the Major didn't know that I would, miraculously, be here. Now listen, Guy. The people here are far too busy to be able to take care of you."

"I think not, Father," Chambrun said from behind us.

Chambrun is short, stocky, with heavy pouches under bright black eyes. Someone was once going to do a movie about the Beaumont. I was asked if I could suggest an actor who would be right for the Chambrun role. Unfortunately, the perfect actor for the part was no longer available. I was thinking of the late Claude Raines. He had Chambrun's elegance of movement and graceful style.

"I'm Pierre Chambrun, son," he said.

Young Guy Willis rushed to him, clung to him. This was someone he could believe in—because his father had told him he could.

The priest made a little gesture of resignation. "Only trying to be helpful," he said. "I'd like to check back with you in a while, Mr. Chambrun, to find out if Ham Willis has turned up safe and sound."

"Do that," Chambrun said. His arm was around the boy, and this gesture was not resisted.

"Will I be able to get through to you?" the priest asked.

"I'll leave instructions to make sure that you can," Chambrun said.

The priest smiled at the boy. "I'm sure there'll be a perfectly normal explanation, Guy. A message miscarried. Someone your father counted on dropped the ball. Good night, gentlemen."

We watched the priest walk out of the Blue Lagoon and into the lobby.

"Let's sit down, Guy, and you tell me what the problem is. I only got a sketchy notion from Mark," Chambrun said. We sat down at the table. "Your parents decided to come down here to listen to the music and left you up in 17C?"

"Yes, sir."

"Was that kind of thing usual?"

"Well, they weren't going anywhere—just downstairs," Guy said. "All I had to do was pick up the phone if I wanted anything. I had a TV set if I got bored."

Chambrun looked up at Cardoza. "Did they reserve a table?"

Cardoza shook his head.

"They talked about it," the boy said. "Dad thought, for the early show at nine o'clock, they wouldn't need a reservation. If he was wrong, they'd come right back. Rozzie laughed and said it would add to the excitement not to be sure."

"Rozzie?"

"My mother, Rosalind."

"Were you pretty full at nine o'clock?" Chambrun asked Cardoza.

"Almost full," Cardoza said. "A couple of side and corner tables left. We were booked solid before Duke Hines was halfway through his first show."

"Could Major Willis and his wife have come in without a reservation, taken one of those side or corner tables without your knowing who they were?"

Cardoza shrugged. "You know our policy, Mr. Chambrun. You set it! When we're that full we don't give the last vacancies to strangers without reservations. We save them for regulars who may just walk in."

Chambrun looked at the boy. "Was your father wearing civilian clothes, Guy, or was he in uniform?"

"Uniform," the boy said. "Dad always wears his uniform when he's not on duty."

Chambrun's dark eyebrows lifted. "Wears a uniform when he's *not* on duty? That suggests he might wear civilian clothes when he *is* on duty."

The boy nodded, as though there was nothing complicated about that. "Dad is in Air Force Intelligence," he said. "When he's on duty he doesn't want to be readily spotted. May I ask you a question, Mr. Chambrun?"

"Of course."

"Isn't it unusual for a priest to be carrying a gun in a shoulder holster?" the boy asked.

Chambrun's eyes narrowed. "Father Callahan?"

"Yes, sir. When he put his arm around me, tried to make me go with him, I wrestled free, pushed away from him. I felt the gun under his left arm then."

"How in the world would you know it was a gun?" I heard myself ask him.

"Dad wears one all the time when he's on duty," the boy said. "I know just what it feels like."

"Why didn't you mention it at the time?" Chambrun asked.

The boy's eyes narrowed. "I was afraid if I did he might decide to use it," he said.

Chambrun's face was suddenly a dark thundercloud. "Mark, see if the Father is still loitering around in the lobby. Guy and I will be up in my office."

THERE WAS NO SIGN of the gun-toting priest in the lobby area. Mike Maggio, the night bell captain, hadn't noticed him, but there was no particular reason he should have, what with people coming and going. Waters, the doorman on the Fifth Avenue side, thought he remembered seeing a priest leave the hotel.

"Short time ago," Waters said. "I had no reason to pay special attention. He just walked away. A priest is a priest is a priest." Waters grinned at me. "Plenty of people in the hotel who need to confess their sins. A priest wouldn't be an attention-getter."

Chambrun's office on the second floor is more like an elegant living room than a place of business—Oriental rug, beautiful antiques, a blue Picasso on the wall opposite The Man's carved Florentine desk, a gift of the artist himself. When I got there to report on the vanished priest, Chambrun's key people were there with him and young Guy Willis. Jerry Dodd, dark, wiry former FBI agent who heads our security, was taking notes. Betsy Ruysdale, secretary extraordinary, lovely to look at with dark red hair, was sitting on the couch opposite Chambrun's desk with the boy beside her. I happen to know that the number where I'd reached Chambrun earlier was Betsy's unlisted phone in her apartment, just east of the hotel.

I reported that Waters had seen a priest leave the hotel. It could have been our man, it could have been some other priest.

"Guy is about to tell Jerry about his evening," Chambrun said. His eyes narrowed against the smoke from one of his Egyptian cigarettes. At his elbow was a demitasse of Turkish coffee, always ready for him in a coffee maker on the sideboard.

"Where is your home, Guy?" Jerry asked the boy.

"It's an apartment in Washington, D.C.," The boy gave an address, which Jerry wrote down.

"This was a pleasure trip, coming to New York?"

"Partly," the boy said. "It was a pleasure trip for me and for Rozzie, my mother. For Dad it was part of his job. Rozzie planned to do some lady-type shopping. I could go to a ballgame at Yankee Stadium. I have a seat for tomorrow's doubleheader."

"Do you know what your father was here to do?"

"His job," the boy said.

"Which is—?"

"Dad's in the Air Force Intelligence," Guy said. "He doesn't talk to Rozzie and me about it because it's top-secret stuff. Star Wars, I think. 'What you don't know, no one can try to force you to tell them,' Dad always tells us."

"Last night they decided to go down to the Blue Lagoon to hear Duke Hines play the piano, leaving you in 17C?"

"Yes, sir."

"And before they left they told you if you had any trouble you were to call Mr. Chambrun?"

"No, sir. I mean, not then. That was when we first checked in, a couple of days ago." The boy glanced at Chambrun. "Dad told me about the thing with the people who attacked you out on the street, sir. He said he felt he could ask you for help if there was any trouble."

"He was right," Chambrun said.

"What kind of trouble did he expect?" Jerry asked the boy.

"I'm just eleven years old, sir," Guy said. "I was going to be pretty much on my own in the daytime. Rozzie would be shopping, no way to reach her; Dad would be doing whatever he was scheduled to do, no way to reach him. I would be going to a ballgame, or the movies or something. I suppose there could be an accident on the street, or at the ballpark, or something. If I needed someone and I couldn't reach Dad or Rozzie I should feel free to call Mr. Chambrun."

"So last night they left you to go down to the Blue Lagoon?"

"Yes, sir. They said they'd be gone for just an hour or so."

"But it was after one in the morning when you tried to find them," Jerry said.

The boy gave him a sheepish look. "I was watching TV, an old Clint Eastwood western. I'd seen it before. I—I fell asleep."

"When you woke up your parents weren't there?"

"No, they weren't, sir, and I was instantly very frightened. Dad had said they'd be back in an hour or so, give or take fifteen minutes. They'd been gone more than four hours when I woke up. Dad would never be that late and not call."

"But you were asleep," Jerry said.

"I was sitting right by the phone in the sitting room, sir. It would have waked me if it had rung. And if it didn't wake me Dad and Rozzie would have come directly up to the suite from wherever they were to find out what was wrong, why I hadn't answered."

"They were having such a good time they didn't notice the way time had passed," Jerry suggested.

"No, sir—not if they were just having fun listening to Duke Hines. When an hour and fifteen minutes went by Dad would have called—if he could!"

Chambrun's coffee cup made a clicking sound as he put it down in the saucer. "Why couldn't he?" he asked.

"Trouble connected with his job," young Guy said. The corner of his mouth twitched as he fought to keep his cool. "He couldn't always tell us, Rozzie and me, when he was coming home. His job isn't like an office job with regular hours. And it's dangerous. That's why he carries a gun. But he keeps in touch when he can, and if he can't make it at a time he's named, he calls—always! When I woke up and he hadn't called, I knew there was some kind of big trouble."

"Do you know who your father's commanding officer is in Washington?" Chambrun asked.

"Steve Martin," Guy said. "Colonel Steve Martin in the Pentagon."

"Did your father have a private number for him?"

"I suppose he may have, sir."

"Would it be up in 17C?"

"I doubt it, sir. It would be private, and it would probably be in his wallet, which he's carrying."

Chambrun pushed back his desk chair and stood up. "Ruysdale, take Guy up to my penthouse and stay there with him, will you?" When it's business he neuters Betsy by calling her "Ruysdale." "Jerry, take Ruysdale and the boy up there, then put penthouse security into effect. After that, a top-to-bottom search for Major and Mrs. Willis.''

''Penthouse security'' meant that the two elevators that go to the roof would be cut off at the floor below. There are three penthouses on the roof, one occupied by Chambrun, one by a fabulous old lady in her eighties named Victoria Haven, and the third held in reserve for special diplomatic dignitaries or famous movie stars who want their stay at the Beaumont to go unpublicized. I happened to know that Penthouse Number Three was unoccupied that night. So the elevators would be stopped at the thirty-ninth floor, guards would be stationed on the fire stairs, and no one would be able to get up to the roof without an okay from Chambrun—or Jerry Dodd. A ''top-to-bottom'' meant a search of every inch of space in the hotel for Major Willis and his wife, no matter how irritating that might be for hundreds of guests who had already retired for the night.

Chambrun put his hand on the boy's shoulder. ''I'll join you in my quarters when I've been able to contact your father's boss,'' he said. ''You're quite sure, Guy, that there wasn't any misunderstanding between you and your folks?''

''Positive, sir. My dad would never leave me hanging out to dry.''

Chambrun patted his shoulder. ''We'll do everything we can to find him, Guy. Keep your chin up. And don't let Ruysdale persuade you to play gin rummy with her. She's unbeatable.''

''Yes, sir.''

LOCATING Colonel Steve Martin in Washington was not easy. Whoever answered the telephone in the Pentagon didn't choose to be cooperative at first. He wouldn't give Chambrun a home phone for Colonel Martin. The next morning after ten o'clock would be the time to make a call. Chambrun could sound like a Good Samaritan or a hanging judge, and he chose to play the latter role. He wasn't calling to ask the Colonel for a favor, rather to do him one. Major Willis, one of the Colonel's men, was in big trouble. If that didn't matter to the Colonel...

The man on the other end said he would contact Colonel Martin and if the Colonel chose, he would call Chambrun. Chambrun gave the man a number—his private phone, not the hotel switchboard.

"If you start waking people up in their rooms at two-thirty in the morning, there's going to be hell to pay," I said.

"You know how long it will take to search every room in this hotel, Mark? Too damn long, but it must be done. Security will go to sleeping quarters last of all."

"You don't think the boy is stirring up a tempest in a teapot?" I asked. "A message miscarried, the boy misunderstood what his father promised him as to a return time?"

"You heard his story. Did you think the boy was hysterical?"

I had to admit I didn't.

"I've lived my professional life trusting my instincts about people," Chambrun said.

"The kid's eleven years old, probably with an eleven-year-old's imagination," I said, playing devil's advocate.

"Ham Willis told his son he and the boy's mother would be gone an hour—fifteen minutes one way or the other. The kid felt so safe he fell asleep. Four hours later Willis hadn't appeared or checked with young Guy about a change in plans. Out of character, cause for alarm quite real."

"All kinds of unexpected things can happen in a big city," I said. "A mugger, a hit-and-run driver, a face-to-face with an old friend you haven't seen for years."

"But this is a special man," Chambrun said. "Anyone can be a target for a mugger. I was, and Ham Willis saved my bacon. But that was outside the hotel. Willis and his wife didn't plan to leave the hotel. Muggings don't happen inside the Beaumont. Neither do hit-and-run drivers cruise through our lobby. Meet an old friend and the Willises decide to stay out longer, they call the boy. Willis is in Intelligence. The boy said 'Star Wars.' Doesn't that raise a few prickles on the back of your neck, Mark? We are a headquarters for friends and foes of the United States, all under the umbrella of the United Nations. I'm suggesting that Major Willis came face-to-face, not with an old friend, but a dangerous enemy."

"Just because he's stayed out later than he originally planned?"

"Because he is what he is, he wouldn't change his plans without notifying the boy."

The private phone on Chambrun's desk rang. It is connected to a squawk box which, when operating, makes the phone conversation audible to whoever else is in the office. Chambrun switched on the box and answered the phone.

"Pierre Chambrun here."

A cold, impersonal voice came through the box. "This is Colonel Steve Martin, United States Air Force. You called me, Mr. Chambrun?"

"I did. Let me tell you, Colonel, before we talk, that one of my trusted people is listening in on this call."

"Get him off," the cold voice said.

"No point," Chambrun said. "Whatever we discuss I will repeat to him later. He might as well hear it firsthand."

"You talk, then," Colonel Martin said.

Chambrun sketched out the story of Major Willis's disappearance and young Guy Willis's concern.

"So Willis was having a good time and forgot to call the boy," Martin said.

"I don't think so, Colonel. To begin with, the Major, wearing his Air Force uniform, never went to the Blue Lagoon, the nightclub he was supposed to be headed for. There was the gun-toting priest who stinks to high heaven. Willis is your man and your problem, Colonel. He happens, also, to be a friend to whom I owe a debt. I'm doing everything that can be done here to locate him. But I'm afraid it may all involve information about which I have no knowledge, dangers which are beyond my control."

There was a moment of silence. Colonel Martin's voice was a little less icy when he spoke again. "Thank you for alerting us, Mr. Chambrun. I'm sending a man to go into detail with you. He's in New York and should be with you in a half hour, forty-five minutes. His name is Clinton Zachary. He is an Air Force officer and he will approach you as a civilian. I'm giving you a number where you can call me. You will be put through at any time. Thanks again for calling."

He gave us a number in Washington and that was that.

TWO

REPORTS BEGAN to trickle in from the hotel's security people. No one had seen an Air Force major in uniform, accompanied by an attractive lady or anyone else, all evening. Willis and his wife appeared to have been the invisible couple. The elevators serving the seventeenth floor at nine o'clock that evening had not been on self-service. That meant the Willises could not have reached the lobby without being noticed by one of our employees. There must have been dozens and dozens of people milling through the lobby at that time of night who weren't guests of the hotel and who had no way of knowing that we would be looking for someone wearing an Air Force uniform who might have been circulating when they were.

"But our people are always watching who comes and goes," Chambrun said when I pointed that out to him. "And they knew what Ham Willis means to me. A special reason to notice him."

Nothing came our way but negatives for the next thirty-five minutes, and then Mike Maggio, the night bell captain, appeared in the door to Chambrun's office.

"A Captain Zachary to see you, Boss," Mike said. "Jerry Dodd said to bring him straight to you."

Zachary, wearing a plain gray tropical-worsted suit, was somehow impressive. His dark hair was crew cut, his gray-blue eyes narrowed and intense. He moved with the lithe grace of an athlete. I wouldn't have wanted to be faced by him in a tight situation. I felt reassured. This man wasn't any kind of stuffed-shirt brass.

"Colonel Martin told you to expect me," Zachary said, his voice cold, clipped.

"Come in, Captain."

"Let's get out of the habit of calling me 'Captain' while I'm on this case," Zachary said. "Colonel Martin gave me a sketchy account of what is supposed to have happened here. It isn't much."

"The Willises left their eleven-year-old son in their suite, 17C, to go down to our nightclub, the Blue Lagoon. The boy expected them back in an hour. He fell asleep watching television and when he woke at one o'clock his parents hadn't returned. The boy had been told to call me if he found himself in any trouble."

"I know about your experience with Willis and some Arab terrorists," Zachary said. "It's in his record file."

"So you understand why I have taken an active role in this as soon as I was notified," Chambrun said.

"Willis talked to you when he checked in?" Zachary asked. "Told you the boy might be left alone and need help?"

"As a matter of fact, we had only the briefest telephone conversation," Chambrun said. "He was busy, I was up to my ears. We made a date to have lunch here in my office tomorrow—today, that is."

"He mentioned that he'd given your name to the boy in case there was trouble?"

"No, which suggests that he didn't anticipate any trouble, doesn't it?"

"In our business—intelligence—you can't anticipate anything *but* trouble," Zachary said. "Let me just say this, Mr. Chambrun. Willis has access to highly classified information that enemies of this country would give an arm and a leg to get. Willis could be a target for any kind of terror tactics imaginable that might force him to tell what he knows."

"The boy mentioned Star Wars."

"Not far off target, I think," Zachary said. The grim lines at the corners of his mouth deepened. "There are always two sides to every coin. Willis could be tortured into giving away vital secrets. He could also be persuaded to sell them for the right price."

Chambrun's face showed his surprise. "Are you suggesting treason?"

"It may surprise you, Mr. Chambrun, to know that something like four hundred thousand people have access to some level of classified information. We're supposed to check out on them, but it would take an army to cover them all more often than once every five years. Some carefully screened people get to know about really high-level stuff. Willis was one of those. But who knows what turns an apple bad in the barrel?"

"You're suggesting that Willis, tested and trusted, is selling out on you?"

"I have to look at both sides of the coin," Zachary said. "Willis can have, somehow, been abducted by the enemy. Or he can have gone bad, sold us out, and taken a powder before we could know he was gone."

"Leaving the boy behind him?"

Zachary's thin lips tightened. "Perfect screen if he wanted us to believe he'd been abducted. No? Boy in on the act, and perfectly safe with a grateful Pierre Chambrun ready to play ball. I'd like to talk to the boy as quickly as possible."

CHAMBRUN, ZACHARY, AND I signaled for an elevator on the second floor. A specially wired button would indicate to the operator that it was Chambrun buzzing and that he should direct any passengers he had on to take another elevator. The door opened and we stepped into an empty car, empty except for the operator, a kid named Eddie Naples.

"All the way, Eddie," Chambrun said, and we started up.

Chambrun and Eddie and I knew that we wouldn't go "all the way." Rooftop security was in effect. The car would stop at the thirty-ninth floor, one down from the roof, the elevator door would open, and an armed security man would check on us. Get the right word from Chambrun and that security man would throw a switch outside the car that would let it proceed to the roof.

It happened just that way. We stopped at thirty-nine, the door slid open, and Captain Zachary found himself looking at a short-barreled automatic rifle aimed straight at his stomach.

"What the hell!" Zachary said.

"All okay, Mr. Chambrun?" Dick Matson, the security man, asked.

"Okay," Chambrun said.

I knew the code. I knew that if Chambrun had answered, quite casually, "All okay," it would have meant he was under duress from the passenger. Just "Okay" meant it really was okay. The elevator door closed, and we went up one more floor to the roof. Chambrun explained the precaution but not the code to Zachary as we walked across the roof to his penthouse, lights shining brightly in the windows. I knew Betsy Ruysdale would have chain-locked the front door on the inside. Chambrun didn't even bother with his key, just rang the bell. After a moment or two the little observation window at the top of the door slid open and we were seen. Then Betsy opened the door.

Chambrun introduced Zachary. Betsy was smiling at the man. "You should have warned *me* not to play gin rummy with that boy," she said. "He's a whiz at it."

We walked into the living room. Young Guy Willis was sitting at a card table. He and Betsy had been using poker chips for money, and most of them were piled up in front of the boy. He left them the moment he saw Chambrun, slid off his chair and came toward us.

"You know something, Mr. Chambrun?" he asked.

"I'm afraid not, Guy," Chambrun said. "This is Captain Zachary. He's in your father's department in the Air Force. Colonel Martin sent him here."

The boy's pale blue eyes narrowed. "Would it be impertinent to ask you your first name, sir?" he asked Zachary.

"Clinton," the Captain said.

The boy seemed to relax. "My father has mentioned you, sir. Do you know something that explains what's happened?"

"Not yet," Zachary said. "But I came up here to find out if you could help me."

"I wish I could, sir."

"So let's sit down and talk about it," Zachary said. He sat down next to the card table, twisted the goose-necked lamp beside it so that the light would shine directly in young Guy's face. Police tactics, I thought.

"Do you know what your father's business was on his trip to New York, Guy?" Zachary asked.

"Surely Colonel Martin could tell you that, sir," the boy said.

"Of course he could. I'm asking if you knew?"

"My father never discussed any official business with me or Rozzie, my mother."

"How would you know what your father discussed with your mother in private? They did have some private time away from you, didn't they?"

"Of course," the boy said, in a tone that suggested he thought Zachary must be an idiot. "What I'm telling you is that my father told us both not to ask questions about his official business. What we didn't know we couldn't be forced to tell anyone."

"Has anyone ever asked you questions about your father's business?"

The boy hesitated. "It wasn't any secret that my dad is in Air Force Intelligence," he said. "People would ask me if I knew anything exciting about what he was doing—mostly kids. They love spy stories. But I didn't have anything to tell them."

"Did your parents have any friends visit them here in the hotel?"

"There was Mr. Romanov. He lives here in the hotel. He came to say hello almost immediately after we arrived. He was there for cocktails last night—before my parents set out for the Blue Lagoon."

Zachary glanced at Chambrun. "'Mr. Romanov' would be Alexander Romanov, the Russian portrait painter?"

"He did a portrait of my dad," the boy said as Chambrun nodded. "It's in our apartment in Washington. They were friends from some time long ago when my dad was stationed in Moscow."

"This hotel seems a strange place for an artist to live," Zachary said. "There must be better accommodations, studio-type, easily available."

"Happenstance," Chambrun said. "Romy was living in an artist's colony upstate—Woodstock, I think. He came to New York on a visit, stayed here. On the north side of this building there are two rooms with large picture windows. I don't know why they're there. They were there before my time. Romy was assigned to one of them on that visit. He was delighted with it, the light perfect for painting. He got a yearly lease from us and has been there ever since."

"You call Romanov 'Romy'?"

Chambrun shrugged. "We have become friends."

"My dad calls him 'Romy,' too," Guy said. "I guess all his friends call him Romy."

The corner of Zachary's mouth twitched. "This is a perfect place for a secret agent from anywhere," he said. "Close to the United Nations, meet here with anyone without attracting attention. Did your father meet privately with Romanov anywhere, boy?"

The boy stiffened. "Are you suggesting that my dad—"

"I'm asking if he met with Romanov privately."

"If it was private I wouldn't know, would I, sir?" A smart kid, our Guy Willis. He couldn't be handled like a child. "I know Dad and Rozzie were planning to go to his apartment to look at some of his new paintings. I was at the Stadium watching the Yankees play the Red Sox. When I got back they told me I should ask Romy to let me see his new work. It was marvelous, they said. Romy promised he'd arrange it before he went back to Washington."

"When was that to be?"

"In a few days. I don't know exactly what day."

Zachary looked at Chambrun. "You should be able to answer that," he said. "How long was he checked in for?"

"As long as he wanted to stay," Chambrun said. "He told me it was uncertain. I told him 17C was his for as long as he wanted it."

"That's unusual, isn't it, for a place as busy as the Beaumont?"

"I owe him an unusual debt," Chambrun said. "My life!"

The front doorbell rang. Knowing the details of roof security I knew only one of two people could be outside the door without Chambrun being warned in advance. It had to be Jerry Dodd, our security chief, or Victoria Haven, who lived in Penthouse Number Two and was already on the roof. Betsy Ruysdale went to the door, and it was Jerry Dodd. One look at his grim face and I knew something was cooking.

"I've been trying to check out on the B shift," he said to Chambrun. "Most of them are home or out on the town."

Chambrun explained to Zachary. "We work in three eight-hour shifts here at the Beaumont," he told the Air Force captain. "The A shift works from six in the morning till two in the afternoon. The B shift from two in the afternoon till ten at night. The C shift goes from ten at night till six in the morning. The B shift would have been on duty when the Willises left their suite to go down to the Blue Lagoon, but long gone when we started looking for them. Dodd's been trying to locate an elevator operator, a bellboy, a desk clerk—someone who may have seen them."

"I'm afraid I found something I wasn't looking for," Jerry said. "Maintenance people dumping trash in a container in the basement—they found Tim Sullivan there, head smashed in like a rotten pumpkin. Very dead, I'm afraid."

"Damn!" Chambrun said, his voice an angry whisper.

"Who is Tim Sullivan?" Zachary asked.

"Elevator operator on the B shift," Jerry answered. "He was on the west bank of elevators, the one the Willises would have used to leave 17C. But that isn't all I found."

"Let's have it, man," Chambrun said.

"In the same trash container was a uniform of an Air Force major."

There was a little cry from young Guy Willis, and he was suddenly clinging to me, the closest person to him. His fingers bit into my forearms like the claws of a frightened bird.

THREE

PEOPLE WHO didn't know Chambrun well might have thought, cynically, that all that mattered to him was what violence like this would do to the reputation of his precious hotel. The truth is that what he cared for most of all was the welfare of "his people." Major Hamilton Willis was a friend and he owed him a debt, but Tim Sullivan was one of his people, a member of his family. He could have told you at that moment what I had no reason to know until I checked—Tim had a wife named Eileen, a young daughter named Nora, and a cherished son named Patrick. He could have told you what grade in school those kids were in and how they were doing. I suppose he could have told us who their grandparents were and where they lived. Chambrun had that kind of information about hundreds of employees, from dishwasher to board chairman, as readily available to him as the programmed information in a computer. He cared about Tim and he was hurt and angry for him. He owed Major Willis and he would pay his debt by caring for the boy, but Tim had counted on him, on the hotel, to make his job safe and secure, and we had somehow failed him. Revenge isn't a civilized notion, but I knew Chambrun was thinking of it. God help the person responsible for Tim's death if Chambrun caught up with him.

"Homicide?" Chambrun asked Jerry Dodd.

"No question. I've already notified the police," Jerry said.

Captain Zachary was somewhere else. "The uniform?" he asked. "Any way to be sure who it belonged to?"

"Simple," Jerry said. "A nametag sewed into the collar of the jacket, the waistband of the pants."

"Willis?" Zachary asked.

Jerry gave him a sour look. "You were expecting maybe Shirley Temple?"

"But no body?"

"Not yet," Jerry said.

Guy Willis was hanging on to me so tightly it hurt, not physically but out of sympathy for the boy. He was whispering to me, urgently. "Why? Why would they take off Dad's uniform?"

I didn't want to give him the obvious answer. A body dressed in that uniform would be easily identified. A body not wearing it, mangled and tossed away somewhere, might not be so easily checked out. Chambrun was thinking along another line, and I almost thanked him for it—for the boy.

"They couldn't have walked Major Willis out of the hotel in full uniform," Chambrun said. "Raincoat, hat, gun in his ribs, and they could have walked him past Captain Zachary unnoticed."

The boy turned in my arms. "Rozzie—my mom?" he asked.

"We haven't even started to look yet, boy," Chambrun said.

"I want to check out on the Willises' suite," Zachary said. "I'd like the boy with me. It could simplify things."

"The boy stays here," Chambrun said.

"I don't take orders from you, Chambrun," Zachary said. "The boy goes with me, if I have to get a warrant for his arrest!"

"Help yourself," Chambrun said. "Only you'll have to get back up here to serve the warrant."

"You want to get in the way of national security?" Zachary almost shouted.

"I'm only interested in the boy's security," Chambrun said. "His father made me responsible for that. He stays here, protected by me and my people."

"You want to fight the United States government, you must be off your rocker!"

"If the United States government wants to fight me here, in my hotel, they may find they've started World War Three," Chambrun said. He turned to Jerry Dodd. "Let's clear the decks here, Jerry, and go look out for Tim. Get Captain Zachary a key to 17C. He can search the suite to his heart's content, but the boy stays here."

"I've got to talk to the boy!" Zachary protested.

"Here—with me present," Chambrun said.

THERE WAS NO possible way of keeping the grim discovery in the basement a secret, even temporarily. Almost two hours before, the search had begun for Major Willis and his wife and everybody alive and well and circulating in the hotel had been asked for a sighting. Reporters were already on the scene when

Tim Sullivan's body and the Major's uniform were found. On our way down in the elevator to 17C, Zachary asked how long we could keep the press off our backs.

"Turn on a radio," Jerry Dodd said, "and you'll find they already know more than we do."

The housekeeper on seventeen provided a passkey to 17C, and we left Zachary there and went on down to the basement where Tim Sullivan's body was found. There was a swarm of reporters and curious rubber-neckers, but the police had cleared them away from the trash disposal area where Tim's body had been found. There was a familiar figure on hand whose presence, I knew, would please Chambrun. Lieutenant Walter Hardy of Manhattan Homicide, an old friend out of the past, was in charge.

"I seem to turn up here about once a year, Pierre, like Santa Claus—but not so cheerful," Hardy said.

I suppose, like any other city, the Beaumont did have violence at fairly regular intervals. Hardy, a big, broad-shouldered blond man, looked more like a thickheaded professional wrestler than the brilliant investigator he was.

"Sorry to see you, Walter—but glad," Chambrun said.

They had worked well as a team, those two, in the past. Chambrun, intuitive, with an instinct for the truth before he had facts to confirm what he guessed, and Hardy, a dogged, step-by-step investigator, never leaving a stone unturned along the way. Together I thought of them as unbeatable.

"Theories, Pierre?" Hardy asked.

Chambrun, I thought, didn't have anything yet on which to base a theory. I was, of course, wrong.

"Major Willis is the key to whatever has happened here," Chambrun said. "A man with secrets worth any kind of risk for an enemy to take. I don't have any way of knowing how anyone knew what his plans for the evening were—mainly that he was going down to the Blue Lagoon to hear Duke Hines play his piano. But someone knew, I think. When the Major and Mrs. Willis left their suite, there was someone else waiting to take the elevator on seventeen. Once in the car, that someone pulled a gun, took charge. I think, when the Medical Examiner gets through with Sullivan's body, you'll find that a bullet was the cause of death, not the head wounds."

"Already determined," Hardy said. "Forty-five-caliber handgun, right in the center of his forehead. Keep guessing, chum."

"I don't think they want Willis dead. They want him alive so he can reveal the secrets they want so badly. They have him and his wife. They would use her to get him to talk. So it didn't work quickly, at any rate."

"You mean they'd torture his wife in front of him?" Hardy asked.

"Something like that. They knew it might happen sometime, and the lady was prepared to take it if it did."

"Brother!"

"But these monsters realized they had another card to play," Chambrun said. "The boy—Guy Willis.

Harm the boy in front of his father and Willis might sell out the world!"

"So, why didn't they take him?" Hardy asked.

"Guessing again, Walter. I think they took Willis and his wife out of the hotel."

"With everyone watching for them?"

"Not at nine o'clock, Walter. We didn't know anything was wrong until the boy alerted us at one o'clock this morning. They stripped Willis of his uniform and tossed it in that trash bin along with Tim Sullivan's body, covered him with a raincoat, or dressed him in a suit they had ready for him, took both the Willises away in a car they had parked down here in the basement garage."

"So they torture Mrs. Willis for three or four hours to get him to talk?" I could tell Hardy didn't want to believe that.

"I don't like to think of the alternative," Chambrun said.

"What alternative?"

"If the Willises knew this might come sometime," Chambrun said, "they might have been prepared. The lady carried—in a ring or a broach she wears—a dose of some kind of lethal poison. Rather than subject herself or her husband to some kind of brutality, it is agreed the lady will take the poison."

"I repeat—brother!" Hardy said.

"So then their only chance is the boy. He may already be in my care. They can't just run in and grab him. So we come to a gun-toting priest who didn't make it. Now, if I'll just get careless when I find myself looking for Tim Sullivan's killer—"

"Where is the boy?" Hardy asked.

"Safe—as the saying goes—as a church. In my penthouse, with no one able to get to him."

"All this without a shred of evidence," Hardy said.

"But highly probable," Chambrun said.

"So Sullivan tried to stop the kidnapping and was shot," Hardy said.

"Or he knew the kidnapper, or the man is so distinctive-looking, a description of him would tell someone who he is—you, me, Captain Zachary."

"The Air Force Intelligence guy? Dodd told me about him."

"We haven't exactly hit it off," Chambrun said.

"Everybody wants a medal except a couple of suckers like you and me," Hardy said. "I guess the next step is to search the elevator Sullivan was operating for fingerprints."

"If we're right, all this happened just about nine o'clock," Chambrun said. "That's when the Willises left 17C, according to the boy. Since that time, Walter, hundreds of people have traveled in that elevator. Prints over prints over prints. I suppose you have to check out for the record, but it's a pretty long shot I'm afraid."

Hardy nodded slowly. "How come if Sullivan was killed around nine o'clock no one reported him missing? His relief didn't come on till ten o'clock, I understand."

"I've got a man checking out on that," Jerry Dodd said, speaking for the first time.

"If Sullivan was killed around nine o'clock," Hardy said, "how come his body wasn't found in that trash bin until after two o'clock?"

"Simple explanation for that," Chambrun said. "Hotel's at its busiest until around two in the morning. Maintenance people don't start moving trash around from the various floors, from the private dining rooms and the closed shops, until about two A.M. That trash is brought down here starting then. An hour or so from now, an outside trucking firm comes in and empties this bin, taking its contents away to official dump sites."

It was at that moment that I saw Captain Zachary arguing with one of the cops who was holding back the crowd of reporters and curiosity hounds. I called him to Chambrun's attention.

"Air Force Intelligence is trying to get to us," Chambrun said to Hardy.

The Lieutenant signaled to his man to let Zachary through. Zachary walked straight up to Chambrun, ignoring the rest of us.

"You and I got off on the wrong foot, Chambrun," he said. "You think we could forget it and start over again?"

Chambrun's face was a cold mask. "You need me for something, Captain?"

"We both need each other," Zachary said. "You can tell me how this hotel works, which people of yours are above suspicion. I can tell you about Ham Willis's world, and who might be involved in what's happened to him. The answer to that is the answer to what happened to your man Sullivan."

Chambrun seemed to relax. "We can give it a try," he said.

"You can be helpful in something that seems important to me," Zachary said. "I would like to talk to Alexander Romanov. If I confront him he'll clam up. You're his landlord, his friend. He needs an alibi for the evening. He might give it to you if he's got one."

"You're suggesting that Romy may be a Russian spy? He's lived here, like an American citizen, for two years."

"Any Russian can be a spy if he gets orders from the KGB," Zachary said. "Do what they tell you, or wind up dead or in Siberia."

Chambrun's shoulders moved in a faint shrug. He introduced Zachary to Lieutenant Hardy. "Walter's in charge of the murder investigation," he said.

"I'm trying to protect national security, Lieutenant," Zachary said. "This Russian artist has made himself a friend of Major Willis. It would be duck soup for him to have led Willis into a trap."

"I'll go with you," Hardy said. "We have to find someplace to start."

ALEXANDER ROMANOV'S suite with its north-light windows was on the tenth floor. There are only a half dozen people outside of Chambrun and some of the work force who live permanently in the hotel. There's old Mrs. Haven in Penthouse Two, who bought her penthouse as a condominium long before Chambrun was involved with the hotel. There are four or five older people who have been given space on long-term leases. And there is Romy Romanov, a vigorous man in his midforties with a loud, joyful laugh and a flashing white smile, popular with everyone who works in the hotel—about as unlikely a candidate for a spy as I can imagine.

The four of us—Chambrun, Hardy, Zachary, and I—waited outside Room 1006 for someone to answer the doorbell.

"Sound sleeper," Zachary said.

"It is going on three in the morning," Chambrun said. "I wouldn't want to be disturbed if I were asleep." He put his finger on the doorbell and held it there. If Romy was in his room, he couldn't ignore it forever.

"You can get a passkey?" Zachary asked.

"Of course," Chambrun said.

It wasn't necessary. There was a sound of the lock turning, and the door opened a crack. Romy Romanov scowled out at us. Then he relaxed.

"Pierre! What on earth—?" Romy opened the door a little wider and saw us all. He didn't open up any wider to accommodate us. "It's after hours for a party, Pierre. Do you realize what time it is?"

"I'm afraid I do, Romy. There has been a kidnapping and a murder. Everyone in the hotel will be questioned between now and breakfast."

"Questioned about what?"

"In your case, Romy, the kidnap victims are your friends Hamilton and Rosalind Willis."

"Oh my God! Are they hurt? Is someone demanding ransom! You said murder—?"

Chambrun identified Hardy and Zachary. "There's no use talking out here in the hall, Romy. Let's go in."

Romy blocked the door opening. "I'd rather you didn't," he said. "Give me a minute to put on some clothes and I'll go wherever you like with you."

"There's no point in making it difficult for Mr. Chambrun," a pleasant woman's voice said from inside the room. "I'm not at all ashamed of being found here with you, Romy. After all, I am over twenty-one."

The lady turned on a light switch inside the room and there she was. I knew her instantly, a regular patron of the Beaumont. Pamela Smythe, the computer heiress.

"Mr. Chambrun, Mark—" Her smile was charming. "I don't know these other gentlemen."

She was wearing a flimsy negligee that did nothing to hide a gorgeous figure, golden hair hung down below her shoulders. She seemed totally unembarrassed.

"I'm sorry, darling. I tried," Romy said.

"You've left us hanging on the edge of a cliff, Mr. Chambrun," the lady said. "You mentioned murder."

Chambrun gave it to her straight out. Tim Sullivan, an elevator operator, had been murdered. Ham Willis's uniform had been found in a trash bin in the basement along with Tim's body.

That seemed to convince Miss Smythe that this wasn't some kind of game. Her smile faded. "The Willises' boy?" she asked. "Is he safe?"

"You know the Willises, Miss Smythe?" Zachary asked.

"They're friends of Romy's. They had cocktails with us here—yesterday, wasn't it, Romy?"

Romanov's handsome face had become cold and hard. "You're here, Pierre, because Captain Zachary suspects me of some complicity in this crime."

"What makes you think that?" Zachary asked.

"You're obsessed with the notion that anyone with any kind of Russian heritage is an enemy," Romanov said. "You've been sniffing around my heels for about three years now. You haven't been as clever about it as you imagine, Zachary. Friends of mine pointed you out to me and warned me about you more than two years ago."

"Russian friends?" Zachary asked.

"It may surprise you to know that it was Major Hamilton Willis," Romanov said. "We are friends from twenty years ago when Ham was a military attaché in Moscow. He said you were just doing your job, Captain, and that as long as I wasn't an enemy spy—which Ham knew I wasn't—I had nothing to worry about. 'An American living in Moscow would be under surveillance. It's no different for a Russian here,' Ham said. So what is it you suspect me of, Captain?"

"You have cultivated a friendship with Willis," Zachary said. "You have persuaded him that you can be trusted. If you wanted to maneuver his comings and goings you could, without any trouble. Someone tricked him tonight. Who more easily than a trusted friend? So, where were you at nine o'clock tonight, Romanov? And after that?"

Pamela Smythe stepped forward to stand directly in front of Zachary. "What is the phrase, Captain? 'An officer and a gentleman'? Romy isn't going to want to answer your questions, because he's a nice guy. He isn't going to want to tell you that I've been sharing his bed with him since about six o'clock yesterday afternoon." She turned to Chambrun. "If you check, Mr. Chambrun, you'll find that dinner for two was served in this room about eight o'clock. The waiter who brought it didn't see me. I wasn't, I suppose you could say, dressed for the occasion. I stayed out of sight while the waiter was here, but he must have known there was a woman in the next room."

"How could he know that?"

"Oh, come, Captain! Dinner for two. And I like to think that the perfume I use is not unattractive. Or hadn't you noticed?"

"You're telling us, Miss Smythe, that neither you nor Mr. Romanov have left this suite since six o'clock yesterday afternoon?" Hardy asked.

"Precisely," Pam Smythe said. She smiled at Romanov. "And if I were invited to stay for another twenty-four hours, I'd accept with pleasure." Then back to Zachary. "If I tell you that Romy is an incomparable lover, would that make me a threat to national security?"

"Did you have any reason to know that Major Willis and his wife were planning to go to the Blue Lagoon last night?" Hardy asked.

"As a matter of fact, I did," Romanov said. "They invited me to go with them." He glanced at Pam

Smythe. "I told them I had other plans for the evening."

"But you could have passed on the Willises' plans to someone else who might want to know them," Zachary said.

"I could have, but I didn't," Romanov said. He wasn't smiling anymore. "Ham Willis is my friend. I'm just as eager to find out what's happened to him as you are. I would help if I could, but I can't as long as you waste time trying to tie me into it."

"Can you tell us who might be after classified information that Major Willis may have?" Hardy asked.

"I could give you a list of names," Romanov said, "which, I may add, doesn't include mine. But Captain Zachary can produce that same list out of his files. I suspect certain of my countrymen of working for the KGB, but I'm not involved with them, nor do I share their secrets. I have lived as an American for the last five years, and I think of myself as an American."

"That's what you would say whether it's true or not," Zachary said.

Romanov's patience appeared to be wearing thin. He spoke directly to Chambrun. "If anyone could have an instinct for the truth about me, it would be you, Pierre. Do you think I'm an enemy agent? If you do, kick me out of your hotel. I will have betrayed your hospitality. If you don't, get this clown off my back and let me help you find the Willises."

"I'd like to help, too," Pam Smythe said. "They're such very nice people."

"You'd both be well-advised to stay out of it," Chambrun said. "These people, whoever they are, play for keeps. But—yes, I have a gut feeling about you, Romy. I'm not going to kick you out of the hotel. If Captain Zachary wants to keep on questioning you, I won't prevent it. I am going to join my staff now in trying to find some clue as to how the Willises were spirited away."

"You think they may still be alive?" Romanov asked.

"I think that way because I want to think that way," Chambrun said. "I prefer to assume that I'm on a rescue mission, not searching for dead people." He turned to Hardy. "I'm headed for the basement garage to see if anyone down there remembers anything of importance."

"I'm with you," Hardy said. Then to Romanov, "I have to ask you and Miss Smythe not to leave the hotel until I can get back to you."

"I wouldn't dream of leaving," Pam Smythe said. "The night's still young." She slipped an arm through Romanov's and looked up at him, flirtatiously provocative.

"Brazen bitch!" Zachary said when Chambrun, Hardy, and I were with him in the outside hall.

Chambrun's smile was thin-lipped. "She couldn't avoid being found with Romy," he said. "What was she supposed to say to us? 'I was just waiting for a bus'? I don't think there are any doubts about motives in this case, Captain. It's even possible that Romanov is part of a network of information gatherers for the KGB. But the fact is that he wasn't physically involved with the abduction of the Willises. The lady gives him a perfect alibi.''

"I'd like to be left alone with him with a hot iron up his behind until he was ready to tell us what he knows,'' Zachary said.

Chambrun stopped in his tracks and faced the Air Force man. "You haven't asked me where I was at nine o'clock, Captain. Don't you suspect me? I let Romanov live in my hotel.''

CHAMBRUN MADE IT very clear on the way down to the basement garage how he felt about the situation. He was talking to Lieutenant Hardy, but Zachary and I were there to hear it.

"There isn't any doubt about the motive for the abduction of Ham Willis and his wife,'' he said. "Someone wants information from him that only he has. The boy spoke about Star Wars—information about secret technology for the ultimate destruction of any enemy. There can be a horde of agents involved. My only hope is that someone slipped up somewhere along the way, leaving us a clue as to how the Willises were taken and where they are now. I'm only concerned with finding them before it's too late. Identifying enemy spies is your job, Zachary. Finding Ham Willis is mine. I owe him.''

"If you two would stop arguing with each other, we might have a better chance,'' Hardy said.

"You're right, of course,'' Chambrun said. "Bury the hatchet, Zachary?''

"Do I have a choice?'' Zachary asked.

Later I knew that Chambrun was hoping that the Willises were being held somewhere in the hotel. Willis, a man of real courage, would have been difficult to get out of the hotel in front of people who would be watching, no matter how casually. You didn't get a car out of the basement garage without involving an attendant. You checked a car in, were given a ticket, and the car was parked for you by an attendant. You didn't get it out without presenting that ticket, when an attendant would deliver the car to you. All Willis would have to do was shout at the attendant that he was being taken away against his will. He would know that if he and his wife were taken away, they were as good as dead.

"Or he would take the chance that by spilling the beans to these people when they got him away he might save his wife, if not himself," Zachary said.

"I don't think so," Chambrun said. "I think they were prepared every day of their lives for that kind of emergency. I suggested before how Mrs. Willis might be prepared."

"But if you search the hotel from top to bottom, as Jerry Dodd is doing—" Hardy said.

"Needle moving around in a haystack," Chambrun said. "There can be half a dozen of these KGB people registered in the hotel under phony identities. We search a room, move on, and the Willises are moved to a room or suite we've already searched and won't go back to. But if that isn't it, garage attendants who were on at nine or ten o'clock may have something for us."

"If they do, then we have a whole city to search," Hardy said.

"Then we've had it," Chambrun said.

"Let them take the boy, stick close, and maybe we haven't," Zachary said.

"Nobody's going to take that boy," Chambrun said. "That's what I really owe Willis. He trusts me to make sure that doesn't happen."

"If Willis is willing to give away military secrets, why protect his boy?" Zachary asked.

"Willis and his wife are ready to hold the fort unless we provide the enemy with a weapon—the boy," Chambrun said. "That I'm not going to do, whether you like it or not, Captain."

Garage attendants on the A and B shifts had been found and returned to the hotel. Not one of them was missing. There were a dozen men who'd been on the job at the critical time. It was difficult to get to ask them questions, they were so full of their own. Tim Sullivan's murder was what concerned them. Chambrun finally got them quieted and ready to answer his questions.

"There is no way the Willises could have been walked out of the hotel through the lobby and to a waiting car or taxi," Chambrun said. "If they were taken away from the hotel, it seems to us it had to be down here, in a car parked in the garage."

Dick Matson, the gray-haired foreman of the garage operation during the busy hours of the evening, had held his position for long before I ever went to work for Chambrun. The underground world of the parking garage was his special province, and he was proud of its efficiency.

"Nine o'clock at night is one of our busiest times," he said. "People leaving after dinner, people coming in for the evening's fun. My guys wouldn't be liable to notice anything special unless there was a commotion."

"And no commotions last night?" Chambrun asked.

"Not that were reported to me—and it would be," Matson said.

"Explain to Lieutenant Hardy and Captain Zachary just what the routines are down here, Dick," Chambrun said.

"We aren't lit up down here like a stage set, as you can see," Matson said. "The entrance is across the way—over there at the north side of the building. The person wanting to park drives in. An attendant approaches him, asks when the owner expects to check out, gives him a claim check, and takes over the car. There's a platform or walk over there like the one we're standing on here. The owner leaves on foot for the elevators that will take him up into the hotel. When he's ready to leave, he comes down to this side." Matson pointed. "There's a cashier's window over there. The owner pays for whatever time he owes, walks out here, and gives his paid claim check to an attendant, who gets his car for him. When the car is delivered here, the owner takes over. He drives out over there, stopped by a security guard who checks his paid claim check and turns him loose."

"So if a man was being taken out at gunpoint, he'd have several chances to ask for help," Hardy said.

Matson nodded. "At the cashier's window, to the attendant who gets the car, to the guard at the exit who gives them final clearance."

"A lot of people who park here regularly must be familiar to you," Zachary said.

"I suppose there are hundreds of them, but we don't know most of them by name. Of course, if it's a well-known movie star, or a politician who gets on TV a lot, we know his name. But let me tell you, Captain, a big percentage of the cars that are parked here are driven by chauffeurs."

"They don't park their own cars?"

"No one drives a car inside this place, beyond the entrance gate and to the exit, except a trained attendant. We'd have a traffic jam forever if we let it be any other way."

"But you know a lot of them?"

Dick Matson grinned at the Captain. "The good tippers we remember."

"They get better service?" Zachary asked.

Matson glanced at Chambrun. "Everybody gets the same service. The good tippers get remembered with a wider smile, that's all."

"There had to be at least four people in the car we're looking for," Hardy said. "Probably five. Major Willis and his wife, a driver for the car, and two men holding guns on their prisoners. Wouldn't your people be likely to remember a group like that?"

"I can check it out," Matson said. "It would be noticeable because mostly just a driver picks up a car.

If he has passengers, he drives out to the front entrance of the hotel and picks them up there."

"Almost certainly these people wouldn't have had the Willises hanging around the front entrance, in the main stream of traffic," Chambrun said. "Check it out, Dick. See if anyone remembers a woman and four men coming down here to pick up a car."

"Could be two women and three men," Zachary said. "No reason an extra woman couldn't have been involved."

Not to make it a matter of suspense, I can report here that Matson couldn't find an attendant who had served any such group leaving the garage area from nine o'clock the night before until now, which was about three in the morning. This tended to support Chambrun's theory—or was it a hope?—that the Willises were being held somewhere in the hotel.

Zachary wasn't buying. "These people aren't dummies," he said. "They could have had more than one car parked down here. One man takes out Major Willis—just two people. Later another one takes out Mrs. Willis. Just two! Two people wouldn't be so unusual coming down here to take off, would they, Matson?"

Matson had to admit that two people coming down for their car after a night of fun in the hotel wouldn't have attracted any particular attention.

"You go to your church, Zachary, which is the whole city of New York," Chambrun said. "I'll stay in mine, which is the Beaumont. There's just a chance we could still get lucky here."

CHAMBRUN TOOK OFF to locate Jerry Dodd and give the orders that would have hotel security rechecking on the areas they'd already checked, on the theory that the kidnappers could have thought of moving the Willises to a place that had already been cleared. Before he left, he had orders for me.

"I want you to go up to the penthouse, Mark. I don't want that boy left with anyone but you or Betsy. And Mark, one of the worse dangers for us in this kind of situation is fatigue. You and Betsy have been going full speed ahead since you came to work yesterday morning—seventeen, eighteen hours. One of you needs some rest."

"How about you, Boss? You've been going as long as we have."

"My motor hasn't started to run down yet," Chambrun said. "In my case someone I really care for is in bad trouble. I couldn't sleep if I tried. Check it out with Betsy. One of you take three or four hours off and then relieve the other one."

"I'll give Betsy the first crack at some shut-eye," I said. "You'll need her more than you'll need me as the day wears on."

"I hope to God I won't need either one of you as the day wears on," Chambrun said. "If we don't find Ham Willis and his wife in a very short time—" Chambrun's shoulder shrug had a kind of angry jerk to it. "Young Guy Willis is important to me, Mark. Treat him as if he was my own kid."

When roof security is in effect, I am one of three people who can get by the blockade without a direct order from Chambrun, the others being Betsy and

Jerry Dodd. The lights were still burning in the living room windows of Chambrun's penthouse when I came out onto the roof. I have a key, so I let myself in without ringing the doorbell.

"Is that you, Mark? Or is it Jerry?" Betsy called out from the living room. She had a special way, apparently, of sensing that it wasn't Chambrun. In passing, let me say that it has been said of me, not too kindly, that I fall in love forever every few months of my life. Perhaps the reason for that is that the woman I could really be in love with forever is beyond my reach. If the man in Betsy Ruysdale's life had been anyone but Pierre Chambrun, I would have been full speed ahead and damn the torpedoes.

There is something about a tired woman—the dark shadows under the eyes, the suggestion that resistance is low—that makes her particularly sexy for me. That's how Betsy looked to me in the early hours of that morning, but it was no time for dreaming.

"All okay?" I asked, looking around for the boy.

"In the guest room," Betsy said. She smiled. It was a tender smile, but for the boy, not me. "I lost over four million dollars to him playing gin rummy. Pierre should have warned me, not him. But I found a way to pay him off."

"Oh?"

"He will call it quits if I don't tell anyone but Pierre and you that I found him crying."

"I'm flattered, but why am I honored with this information?"

"He trusts you. You got Mr. Chambrun for him when he was in trouble. There's no reason that people you trust shouldn't know your weaknesses."

"Weaknesses?"

Betsy smiled again, this time for me. "A man doesn't cry when he's frightened. It would be shameful for anyone else to know except the people he trusts."

"Poor kid," I said. "He's scared for his parents, and I'm afraid he has every right to be."

"It's that, and something more," Betsy said. "I persuaded him to try to nap. He'd only been down for a short time when I heard him screaming. I rushed into the bedroom and found him sitting bolt upright in bed, sobbing. It had been nightmare time."

"Not surprising, considering what he's been through."

"What bothered him most was that I'd caught him acting like an eleven-year-old kid," Betsy said.

"Which is what he is."

"He doesn't think of himself that way," Betsy said. She laughed. "Anyway, I canceled my multimillion-dollar loss by promising not to tell anyone but you and Pierre."

Betsy and I didn't have too much of an argument about who should take the nap. Chambrun would need her when the regular day started in the hotel. She could handle the business of the hotel almost as efficiently as he could. He wasn't going to have time for anything but a murder investigation—unless it had been solved and the Willises were accounted for.

"Guy has dozed off again," Betsy told me. "Just be where he'll know you're here if he has another nightmare. I'll leave a call for seven-thirty. Relieve you by eight."

I took a look into the guest room when Betsy had left. The boy was there, his blond head turning restlessly on the pillow. He must be dreaming again, I thought. Even as I thought it, he sat straight up in bed, saw me outlined in the doorway, must have thought for a minute that something had happened to Betsy and that I was a stranger. His hands went up to his mouth as if to stifle a cry.

"It's okay, Guy," I said. "It's Mark Haskell."

He lowered his hands. "Oh, wow! For a minute I thought it was—"

"Dreaming again?"

"Betsy told you?"

"Yes. She's gone to take a snooze."

"I—I was so ashamed," the boy said. "To be crying just over a dream!"

"Dreams are sometimes scarier than the real thing," I said.

"Oh, boy!"

"You want to tell me what it was? It may help you forget it."

His lips were trembling, and I realized he was fighting tears again. "It was my mom and dad," he said, his voice shaken. "They were lying side by side on the ground. I couldn't tell if they were tied there or—or if they were dead. And—and there were two men beating them with clubs—or maybe baseball bats. And—and there was blood everywhere. Their—their faces were all smashed to a pulp, but I knew they were Roz-zie and Dad.''

"Ugly, but a dream," I said.

He looked at me, and tears had welled up in his eyes again. "One of the two men with the bats was facing me, and I could see who he was—that priest, Father Callahan. The other one had his back to me, and I never did see his face, but somehow—somehow I was sure that I knew him. I'm still trying to think who it could have been, because—because I was just starting to dream it all over again. I started screaming, sat up, and there was a man standing in the doorway. It was you, of course, but with the light behind you I couldn't see your face, and for a minute I thought you were the other man who, with the priest, had been beating up on Mom and Dad. Of course, when you spoke..."

I put my arm around him and gave him a little hug. "Dreams are usually pretty easy to trace back," I said. "Something that's just happened to you, or you've seen, or read, or heard. The uncertainty about what's happened to your parents, that gun-toting priest who tried to get you to go away with him, the murder of our Tim Sullivan; I suspect we'd all be having night-mares if we'd had a chance to sleep. You're afraid for your folks, and that makes you dream the worst. It was just a bad dream, Guy. Not real.''

His eyes were wide, looking past me. I realized he was seeing it all again, just as clearly as when he'd dreamed it. His whole body was trembling.

Behind me I heard the front door open. It could only be Chambrun.

"In the guest room," I called out to him.

He wasn't alone; Lieutenant Hardy was with him. I sensed there was something new that brought them both here.

"I'm glad you're awake, Guy," Chambrun said. "There's something I wanted to show you and ask you." He held out his hand, palm up. I saw he was holding a brooch, a gold frame with a large red stone set in it. It looked like a gorgeous ruby. "You ever see this before, Guy?"

"It looks like Rozzie's," Guy said, frowning.

Chambrun moved his fingers and the scarlet stone popped upward, and I saw that it wasn't a stone at all, just a cleverly painted piece of glass that covered a cavity almost as big as the inside of a thimble.

"It's Rozzie's," the boy said. "She showed me how it worked once."

"Did she tell you why she wore it?"

"She said she had it made so she could surprise anyone who got fresh with her."

"Did she tell you what that surprise was?"

The boy shook his head. "She just laughed and said there'd be something in the ring that would surprise anyone who gave her any trouble. I thought it might be something like Mace. I'd heard about that. Some people carry it to throw in the eyes of a mugger if they get attacked on the street."

"Can you remember if she was wearing this when she and your father went out last night?"

The boy shook his head. "I didn't notice particularly. But she always wore it when she went out, like a good-luck charm. I guess I just stopped looking for it when they were going somewhere. I just took it for granted.''

I think I guessed what was coming and wished I could put it off. ''Where did you find it?'' I asked Chambrun.

''Room 17E, the next room on the same side of the corridor as the Willises' suite. Do you know someone named Henry Graves, Guy?''

The boy shook his head. ''I don't think so, sir.''

''A friend of your father's?''

''Gee, sir, Dad has so many friends all around the world that I've never heard of. There was no one named Henry Graves who was an 'at home' friend, a social friend.''

''About eight o'clock last night your father made a phone call to the front desk. Do you remember hearing him?''

''No, sir.''

''Had he left your suite for a while?''

''No, sir. But I was in the living room. He could have made a call from the bedroom phone.''

''Your father told the desk clerk that an old friend of his had arrived in town unexpectedly. He hoped we could find a room for him, preferably near 17C. By coincidence the guest in 17E had checked out earlier than expected. We'd normally have held that room for someone on the waiting list, but everyone knew that I'd want Major Willis given special treatment, so 17E was made available for his friend, Henry Graves.'' Chambrun's eyes focused on the boy. ''Your father didn't mention this friend of his, Henry Graves, to your mother in your presence, Guy?''

"No, sir."

"You say you found that brooch in 17E, Graves's room?" I asked.

Chambrun was obviously thinking way ahead of me. He sounded almost irritated as he answered. "We began the search for Willis and his wife on seventeen, working down," he said. "I gave orders to search again the rooms we'd already checked out."

"The possibility that the Willises could have been moved back to a place we'd already searched?"

Chambrun nodded. "So we started on seventeen again. There was no one in 17E either time we searched."

"But the brooch wasn't there the first time around?"

"Can't be sure," Chambrun said. "We were looking for people, not small objects like this. Second time around one of Jerry's men just happened to see the brooch lying in the corner of the room. It could have been there the first time."

"How does Henry Graves explain it?" I asked. "It certainly suggests that Mrs. Willis was in 17E at some point."

"Mr. Graves doesn't explain it because Mr. Graves is among the missing," Chambrun said. "He wasn't there the first time we searched the room, nor the second."

"When did he check in?"

"Just after eight o'clock, just after Major Willis's phone call to the front desk. Karl Nevers, the chief night clerk, was involved with a group that had just come in from Kennedy Airport. Miss Jacobs handled

Graves's registration. He had no luggage. He told her he hadn't expected to be in town overnight. He said he'd buy himself a toothbrush and borrow a razor and some pajamas from his friend Major Willis."

"Did your father leave some things—a razor, pajamas—for someone to pick up?" I asked Guy.

"No, sir."

Chambrun sat down on the edge of the bed beside the boy. "There is no way to hide certain ugly possibilities from you, Guy," he said. "If I'm not honest with you now you'll hear it all in the morning on the radio, the TV, or read it in the morning papers. I think Henry Graves is a phony, like your priest. I don't think your father called to reserve him a room. No way the reservation clerk could have known that the voice on the telephone wasn't your father's. I think this Graves, whoever he is, maneuvered your parents into his room when they left to go down to the Blue Lagoon. Was able to persuade them to go into 17E."

"Probably at gunpoint," Lieutenant Hardy said.

"Oh, wow!" the boy said.

"What I think your mother carried in that brooch, Guy, was a deadly poison. We'll know for sure presently. There was just a trace of it left in the brooch, and the police lab is testing it out now."

"Why would Rozzie carry poison?" Guy asked.

"I don't know this for sure, Guy, but I think she had it to use in case someone planned to harm her to get your father to give away secret information."

"How could she get anyone to take it?" Guy asked.

"Not anyone, Guy—herself. She could die painlessly, or at least quickly that way, and not be used to force your father's hand."

"I'm afraid that's why the priest wanted you, boy," Hardy said. "They no longer had your mother to use to force your father to talk."

The boy's whole body shook like a palsy victim. He was hanging on Chambrun's arm as if his life depended on it. "Are you saying that Rozzie—that my mother killed herself?"

Hardy's grim face offered little hope. "I'm sorry, boy."

"But that's in no way certain," Chambrun said, briskly, like a man getting his second wind. "It's a pretty sound guess, I think, that this man who calls himself Henry Graves is not a friend of your father's, Guy. Oh, he may have posed as a friend, even convinced your father that he was a friend. But he was 'the enemy.' As such, he would have studied your father carefully and in detail, his habits, his likes and dislikes, how he might react if it came to a showdown. He might know about that brooch of your mother's and how she intended to use it if it came to it. You think your mother would have the courage to take her own life if the danger was great?"

Tears had surfaced in Guy's eyes once more. "Rozzie would have the courage to do anything she had to do if my dad was in danger or threatened in some way—or if someone planned to use her to make him betray some of the secrets of his job."

"It was understood between your parents?"

"They never talked about it in front of me," Guy said. "But when you suggest it may have been that way, I believe it could have been."

"So your parents had been forced into Henry Graves's room," Hardy said. "Your mother was threatened, or actually attacked in some way, and she took the poison in the brooch."

It was too much for the boy, and he lowered his face against Chambrun's shoulder and wept.

Chambrun gave the boy a cheerful pat on the back. "There are other possibilities, Guy. As I suggested, Graves may have known a great deal of intimate detail about your parents. He may have known about the brooch. When he had your parents under his control in 17E, he may have ripped the brooch off your mother's dress, dumped the poison out of it, and tossed the brooch into the corner of the room. Your mother no longer had her grim method of escape."

The boy looked up, cheeks tear-stained. "Could that be?"

Hardy answered him. "My lab technicians are going over the room now, boy. If they find traces of the poison on the rug, or on a piece of furniture, it would make Mr. Chambrun's explanation likely."

"But if she took the poison, what did they do with her?" Guy asked.

The alternatives were obviously not pleasant to present to the boy. If she had taken the poison and was dead, how had Graves disposed of the body? How could they have taken her out of the hotel, alive, with hundreds of people looking for her? I asked those questions to satisfy my own curiosity.

Chambrun gave me the look of a patient parent trying to deal with a dim-witted child. "You're not thinking, Mark," he said. "Hundreds of people were not looking for the Willises from the time they took off from their suite at nine o'clock to go down to the Blue Lagoon until after one in the morning when Guy notified us that they were missing. That's a stretch of four hours in which no one was concerned about them, looking for them, had any special interest in them. There are more ways than I can think of that they could have been moved around, alive or dead, in that four-hour stretch without attracting any attention."

"How long had Tim Sullivan been dead when he was found?" I asked. "He must have been caught in the middle when they were moving the Willises around. No?"

Hardy answered my question. "The Medical Examiner thought Sullivan had been dead about three hours. He was found around two this morning, which would suggest that he was done in somewhere around eleven o'clock last night. But—that trash bin is as hot as an oven on warm, which makes it impossible to be dead certain. It could have been earlier, later—who knows?"

"It's all my fault!" the boy suddenly cried out. "If I hadn't fallen asleep watching the television I'd have let you know right after ten o'clock that something was wrong. I let them have hours to work on Mom and Dad!"

"You're not to blame at all, boy," Chambrun said. "You weren't told to stay awake, were you? If anyone is to blame, I am. I let this happen to a cherished friend in my hotel!'' Something of the enormous fatigue Chambrun must have felt showed in the deepening lines of his face. He had been on the go since seven-thirty the previous morning, his normal rising time. There had been the pressures of the regular daily routine, then the growing tragedies of this early morning—the murder of a trusted employee, the disappearance and the threat of terminal violence to a friend he owed, now this boy to protect and care for. He looked down at the boy now with something that looked like genuine affection. ''I can't promise you everything will turn out all right, boy,'' he said, ''but I can tell you that every resource I have, every bit of manpower, every ounce of special skills at my disposal will try to make it come out all right. Play it the way I am, Guy. Hope for the best. It can happen, and we'll fight to make it happen.''

Guy still hung on to this man his father had told him to trust. ''If Rozzie took that poison while I was sleeping—''

''If you had warned us at ten o'clock we might have had no better luck than we've had later,'' Chambrun said. ''I've got to check with our security people who are searching. Mark will stay with you. Try to get some sleep. Win or lose, it's going to be a pretty hectic day coming up.''

''Sleep isn't easy,'' I said. ''It's nightmare time.'' I gave Chambrun a brief sketch of Guy's gory dream.

''Try thinking about all the good times you've had with your parents, Guy,'' Chambrun said. ''Perhaps that'll help.''

A FEW MINUTES after Chambrun left me alone with Guy in the penthouse, I began to be aware of how vital sleep was to all of us. The boy, in spite of what must have been a shattering anxiety for his parents, dozed off, twitching and turning on the bed where he lay. It must have been nightmare time again, I thought. I remembered leaning my head back against the chair where I sat and closing my eyes because they felt raw and tired from more than twenty hours without closing. The next thing I knew, early-morning sunshine was streaming through the bedroom window. I glanced at my wristwatch. It was almost quarter of eight. Betsy Ruysdale would be relieving me any minute now. I glanced at the boy. He seemed to be sleeping quietly now.

I tiptoed out into the kitchenette and got the Mr. Coffee machine going. There must not be any news, good or bad, I thought, or I would have heard from Chambrun.

I realized that one of the morning news shows must be showing on TV. I switched on the set in the kitchen, keeping the volume low with the hope it wouldn't disturb Guy. I was suddenly in the lobby downstairs, where Rex Chandler, one of the top newsmen, was interviewing Eleanor Jacobs, the night clerk who had registered the man who called himself Henry Graves. Eleanor looked worn out, probably from answering the same questions dozens of times for dozens of reporters.

"Can you describe this man who called himself Henry Graves, Miss Jacobs?" Chandler was asking her.

"It was about eight o'clock in the evening," Eleanor told him. "It was a hectic moment at the front desk. A bus had just come in from Kennedy with eight or ten people from the West Coast all trying to register and get to their rooms at one time. Mr. Henry Graves got to me to handle his problem. There was a note on his reservation card indicating that he was a friend of Major Willis's and that Mr. Chambrun would want special care for him. Room 17E had been set aside for him."

"But you had a reason to pay special attention to him, didn't you?" Chandler asked.

"Yes and no," Eleanor said. "He didn't have any problems. He explained that he'd found himself in town unexpectedly, had no luggage, would borrow anything he needed from Major Willis. Asked where the drugstore was so he could buy himself a toothbrush."

"His looks, Miss Jacobs? The police and we, the press, are all trying to find him."

"A dark summer suit—dark gray or dark blue, I can't be certain. A gray snap-brim hat with brim pulled down over his forehead. Black glasses—"

"At eight o'clock in the evening?"

"You've been in this business long enough to know, Mr. Chandler, that dark glasses these days are more often cosmetic than medical. Way of staying anonymous for movie stars and other important people."

"Anything else distinctive about him?"

"Nothing. That was it, I guess—the only distinctive thing about him was that there was nothing distinctive! I couldn't see the color of his hair, so it must have been worn short under that hat. Glasses concealed the color of his eyebrows—big round glasses. He was medium tall, just about six feet, I'd say. Not overweight or underweight."

Eleanor had seen more than most people see in a stranger. I suppose it was part of the training for her job. The TV news went from the lobby of the Beaumont to riots in South Africa, and I turned it off. Enough coffee had come through the Mr. Coffee machine for me to pour myself a cup when I heard the front door open. It would be Betsy to relieve me, I thought, and I went out into the living room to greet her.

It wasn't Betsy. It was Chambrun, accompanied by Jerry Dodd. Chambrun was almost unrecognizable. His face was the color of gray ashes in a fireplace. His mouth was a thin knife slit in his face. His eyes were clouded ice. I guessed there was news of the Willises—bad news. It was worse than that, from Chambrun's point of view. He held out a folded sheet of white paper to me, not speaking.

"Came by special messenger," Jerry Dodd said.

There was one sentence typewritten on the piece of paper. "IF YOU WANT TO SEE YOUR MISS RUYSDALE ALIVE AGAIN TURN THE BOY LOOSE."

PART TWO

ONE

I FELT MY LIPS moving, but no sound came.

"Betsy doesn't answer her phone," Jerry Dodd told me. "I've sent a couple of my men around the corner to her apartment to check it out."

Chambrun sat down at his writing desk, pounding at its flat surface with his clenched fists. I slipped out into the kitchen and brought him a mug of coffee. He drinks it round the clock, and I guessed he could use it now. The phone was ringing as I brought it to him. Jerry answered. It was apparently one of Jerry's men reporting to him. He shook his head as Chambrun stared at him.

"Talk to any people you can find in the building." Jerry put down the phone. "She isn't there, Boss. No sign of any violence. My man says it doesn't look as though she slept there. Bed neatly made, just the way she might have left it when she went to work yesterday morning." He turned to me. "What time did she leave you, Mark?"

"Around three-thirty, I think. I know she planned to leave a call for seven-thirty, and I figured she'd get about four hours sleep."

"She may never have gotten home," Jerry said. "Bastards picked her up out on the street."

"So help me," Chambrun said in a shaken voice, "if they have hurt her—!" And he pounded down the desk again with his fists, making the coffee mug I'd brought him bounce.

"You're going to have to tell Lieutenant Hardy," Jerry said.

"This isn't a homicide yet," Chambrun said. "I've got to think—"

"About turning the boy loose?" Jerry asked.

"You want to turn me loose?" It was Guy Willis, standing in the doorway, rubbing at his sleep-swollen eyes.

"Damn!" Chambrun muttered. He hadn't wanted to tell the boy, not yet, at any rate. "He has to know, Mark."

I picked up the threatening note from the desk where Chambrun had dropped it and carried it over to the boy. He read it, his eyes widening.

"They've hurt Betsy?" he asked.

"That's all we know at the moment," I said, indicating the note.

"I don't understand," Guy said.

Chambrun turned in his chair, fighting for control. His voice was almost gentle as he spoke to the boy. "It's like an old joke, Guy—'I have good news for you and bad news.' The good news is that your father is still alive, still unwilling to tell them what they want to know. The bad news is that if they tried to use your mother to get him to talk, they failed. Their last chance is to get you to him, threaten you with bodily harm, in the hope that will break your father down. To prevent that is why you're here, with Betsy and Mark to guard you along with Mr. Dodd's security force."

"So—so they've got Betsy and are threatening to harm her unless you surrender me to them?" Guy asked.

"Something like that," Chambrun said.

"Well—of course, you have to," the boy said.

Chambrun stared at him as though he couldn't believe what he'd heard.

"You can't let them use Betsy, who doesn't even know my dad more than to say hello to, to force Dad to give them what they want. I'm the one that should have to face it—whatever it is."

"Look, kiddo, I don't think you quite understand—" Jerry began.

"Dad wouldn't want me to hide behind a woman's skirt," Guy said.

"I think we all need to face the situation as it really is," Chambrun said. He took a sip from the mug of coffee I'd brought him. "It's very grim, Guy, and very black. You ready for it?"

"Yes, sir."

"Your father has information these people have already committed one murder to try to get—Tim Sullivan. They hoped to use your mother as a means of making your father talk. It hasn't worked, we can only hope not for the very worst reason. Then they tried to get you, using the priest. Now I've got you where they can't get you. So they snatch Ruysdale to force my hand."

"So let them have me, sir," young Guy said. "It's the Willises' problem, not yours or Betsy's."

"But think in terms of the blackest kind of villainy, boy, if you can," Chambrun said. "Your father and mother can identify these people if they ever get free. They'll keep your father alive because only he can give them the information they want so badly. Your mother?'' Chambrun's shoulders moved in a little shrug. "Now they've got Betsy. Will they free her if I meet their demand and set you loose? She could identify some of them, so she can't win. They'll keep her alive as long as they think they can use her to make me give in, turn you over to them. After that they won't dare let her go. Your father is alive, but he must know that whether he talks or not there's no hope for him in the end. As long as I don't set you free, Guy, there's a chance that all of them—your dad, mother, and Betsy—will be kept alive. So we keep you safe here and we have just a little while in which we can hope to catch up with them.''

The boy's lips trembled. "I thought you said the brooch meant that Rozzie had taken the poison.''

"Or been prevented from taking it,'' Chambrun said. "If your father knew she'd killed herself, nothing on earth would persuade him to talk—unless it was you. If your mother is alive, and they start to torture you in front of her, she might persuade your father to talk.''

"And even if he did you'd all be dead ducks,'' Jerry Dodd said. "None of you would ever be let go to identify them to the top brass.''

"That's the way it is, boy,'' Chambrun said. "They'll give us a little time to figure out what our chances are, probably threaten us again, maybe put Betsy on the phone to ask me for help. Then, if I do turn you loose you're all dead, and if I don't all but you are dead."

"I'd want to go with them," Guy said.

"But if I keep you here, protected, it will give us some time—hours, a day—to find some answers and stage a rescue. Cooperate with us, boy. It's the one chance there is for your parents and Betsy."

The boy hesitated, drew a deep breath. "Yes sir. I'll do whatever you say."

IN RETROSPECT it's hard for me to remember the exact sequence of events in the next little stretch of time. Some of them I was in on, some of them I heard about later.

One of our basic problems, as Jerry Dodd pointed out to Chambrun, was manpower. Still playing with Chambrun's theory that the Willises and, possibly now, Betsy were being cleverly hidden in the hotel, moved to safety areas after they'd been searched, Jerry pointed out that we'd need the National Guard to help keep those searched places covered so they couldn't be used again. You could close the hotel, check everybody out, then send in the army. But that was a process that would take hours.

We probably didn't have hours. In the course of such an elaborate move the people holding the Willises and Betsy would be alerted, move with the tide, and disappear. We needed every bit of possible help we could get, and that dictated the necessity of letting Hardy and Captain Zachary in on what had happened to Betsy. That would give us police help and the special knowledge of the armed services intelligence know-how. I was given the job of informing those two potential allies what was cooking while Chambrun and Jerry went around the corner to Betsy's apartment to see for themselves if there was any sort of clue that might help. I don't think Chambrun would have left the hotel in a crisis for any other reason in the world than to help someone as precious to him as Betsy. I didn't believe there was any other such person.

Chambrun had one fresh piece of information before he and Jerry set out for Betsy's apartment. Betsy had told me she was "going to leave a call" for seven-thirty so she could relieve me at eight. There was no special phone service in the little brownstone where she had her apartment, and so the call was left at the Beaumont's switchboard. Ora Veach, the chief operator on duty in the early morning, called Betsy every workday at seven. This time there had been a message not to call her till seven-thirty. Ora Veach informed Chambrun that there'd been no answer when the switchboard called at seven-thirty.

"I figured her routine habits had wakened her before we called," Ora told The Man. "Probably in the bathroom and didn't hear the phone. We tried twice more in the next ten minutes. No luck. I'm sorry, Mr. Chambrun, but I didn't think there was any reason to be alarmed. Habit had waked her ahead of time and she was probably on her way over here."

If she was ever at home at all, Chambrun thought. Jerry Dodd's notion that Betsy had been picked up on her way home was eating at him. It was less than a block from the hotel, a well-lighted street, but deserted at three-thirty in the morning.

There is no doorman or any visible help in the brownstone where Betsy lived. The superintendent cares for several buildings in the area. It didn't surprise Jerry that Chambrun had a key to the front door of the building and another to Betsy's apartment.

"The apartment was neat as a pin," Jerry told me a little later. "Bed made, not even a coffee cup left on a table. I was satisfied that Betsy never got there after she left the hotel."

Chambrun was certain she had been there. "Out-of-character neat," he told Jerry. "And the bed! Betsy didn't make that bed." He explained she had a special way of making the bed, the spread pulled up under the pillow, then doubled back out and up over the pillow. "As automatic as the way you brush your teeth," Chambrun said. "Betsy never made the bed this time."

"Cleaning woman?" Jerry suggested.

"Comes on Fridays—day after tomorrow," Chambrun said. "Betsy was here, sleeping. Somehow they got to her."

"She had to let them in. There's no sign the door was forced."

Chambrun nodded. "They'd have to ring the buzzer outside the front door to this building. Betsy answers. It's someone she knows. Betsy presses the release button that lets them in downstairs, and opens up for them when they get here."

"At four in the morning?"

"Someone claims they have a message from me."

"Would she buy that? You'd phone her, wouldn't you?"

"The way things were boiling at the hotel? In any case, Betsy was flimflammed by someone she knew. I'm guessing there was some kind of physical struggle when Betsy discovered she'd been had, place messed up. When they had her under control, they neatened it up, made the bed."

"Why?"

"There are some men's clothes in the closet, shaving equipment in the bathroom. A boyfriend might be turning up. They didn't want us to know anything had happened to Betsy until they were ready for us to know."

"Betsy has a live-in boyfriend?"

"She certainly does," Chambrun said. "Me!"

I don't think Jerry was remotely surprised by the information, only that Chambrun had gone public with it.

"If it was someone Betsy knew," Jerry said, "then it almost certainly is someone you know."

"I haven't missed that one, Jerry," Chambrun said. "And I can promise you, if Betsy's been hurt, he's not going to be someone I know, but someone I knew!"

While this was going on I was with Hardy and Zachary in Chambrun's office at the Beaumont, bringing them up to date on what had happened to Betsy. They reacted differently. Hardy had come to know Betsy over the years, trusted her, had probably come to like her. He acted as any normal man would to the threat of danger to a friend. To Zachary, however, Betsy was just another piece on the chessboard of a game he was playing. They make a move, we make a move. Until now it seemed to me they had made all the moves.

"I've thought from the beginning Chambrun should let the boy go," Zachary said. "We cover him and are taken right to where they're holding Major Willis. Now, it seems, they've forced his hand."

"Doesn't it occur to you that if they get the boy to his father the classified information you care so much about will be gone?"

"Not if we're right there behind the boy," Zachary said.

"Can you guarantee that?" Hardy asked.

"Can you guarantee anything in your job?" Zachary countered. "In our kind of jobs we just have to play the best card we hold and hope."

"The best card we hold is the boy—kept out of their reach," Hardy said.

"Look, Lieutenant," Zachary said, anger darkening his face. "In your job you want to find a man and punish him for a crime. If you fail, you fail. In my job I'm trying to save a whole nation from disaster. If I fail, that whole nation may go down the drain. Would I risk one eleven-year-old kid for a chance to win? You're damn right I would, and so would you if you'd think about it for a minute."

Hardy didn't react one way or the other. His face was chiseled out of stone. "Who is with the boy now?" he asked.

"Mrs. Haven—Victoria Haven," I said.

Hardy nodded.

"Who is Mrs. Haven?" Zachary asked.

It would have taken a whole book to answer that question. Victoria Haven is the eighty-odd-year-old widow lady who owns and lives in Penthouse Number Two on the roof. She is a tall, still handsome ex-show girl, several times divorced or widowed, with hair dyed a color of red that even God never invented. She lives alone except for what she calls "my Japanese gentleman friend," a nasty-tempered little black-and-white Japanese spaniel. Her penthouse is wildly disordered, a storehouse for mementos from a long and exciting life.

"It looks like disorder," Chambrun once said to me, "but if you want the details of some important news story from fifty years ago, Victoria will just reach out and hand you the clipping. That disorder is complete order as far as she's concerned."

"Chambrun's so concerned about the kid's safety," Zachary said, "that he leaves an eighty-year-old woman to protect him?"

"Mrs. Haven isn't protecting Guy, any more than I was or Betsy. Rooftop security keeps anyone from getting up there without an okay from Chambrun or Jerry Dodd. Like Betsy and me, Mrs. Haven is just there to keep the boy company. Listen to anything he may have to say or may remember that might be useful. Lets him know that he isn't alone and that there is someone who can reach Chambrun, the only person he really trusts."

"How very nice," Zachary said, his voice a sour rasp. "You make sure a kid isn't lonely, when, if properly used, he might lead us to a way to save this country from destruction by the enemy."

"Chambrun sees it another way," I said. "Don't risk letting the enemy use the boy, and your secrets are safe. Major Willis will never cave in under threats or physical torture to himself. Attack the boy in his presence and he just might—"

"A stalemate," Zachary said.

"So neither side wins," Hardy said. "Let's keep it that way until we can figure out how to win."

The office door opened and Chambrun, a man looking dead on his feet, joined us.

CHAMBRUN CAUGHT US up on what Betsy's apartment had revealed. The main conclusion, as far as he was concerned, was that Betsy had let someone she knew and trusted into her apartment and had been double-crossed and betrayed.

"It wouldn't be some friend just interested in fun and games," Hardy said. "Not at four or five o'clock in the morning."

"Not this day, not this particular morning," Chambrun said.

"Someone connected with hotel security, or the police," Zachary said. "A bad apple in one of your barrels."

Chambrun ignored that comment as though he hadn't heard it. There were no bad apples in his barrel. If he wasn't sure of that he would have retired long ago.

"You and Alexander Romanov were talking a while back about lists of possible enemy agents who might be staying here or be regular customers of the hotel," he said to Zachary. "Make your list for me, please,

Zachary." Then, to me, "Mark, go to Romanov and ask for his list. Maybe between the two lists we'll come up with someone that Betsy would know and trust. That would certainly be someone that I, too, would know and trust. If there's such a name on either list, we may have a starting point."

"Don't let Romanov know why you want the list," Zachary said to me. "If you tell him he'll know who to cover for."

"If he deserves your suspicions, Captain, he'll know in advance why we want the list," Chambrun said. "If he doesn't deserve those suspicions, knowing why we want the list may head him in the right direction. Tell him, Mark."

I left the office, hearing Zachary muttering under his breath. He and Chambrun hadn't buried the hatchet after all.

From the outer office I called Romy Romanov's room, and he answered promptly. I asked if I could come up and talk with him.

"Coffee waiting for you," he said. Which reminded me that I hadn't had anything to eat since an early dinner the night before. My stomach was complaining.

Romy was waiting in the open door of his room when I got there. I went in with him and found Pamela Smythe smiling at me from where she was perched in a corner of the couch across the room. She was wearing a nice-looking, pale-blue summer cotton dress—a little more formal than the last time I'd seen her, but not less attractive.

I let them both know what had happened, with nothing held back. Romy exhibited some distress as the story unfolded. Pam Smythe listened, frowning.

"I'll make you a list," Romy said when I'd finished. "It won't be a big one—seven or eight names. It has to be people who know the hotel, who are familiar with Miss Ruysdale. She wouldn't have let a complete stranger into her apartment, no matter what credentials he offered. Give me a few minutes to think." He gave me a bitter little smile. "I suppose Zachary is sure I won't give you any name that'll be of any use to you."

"Something like that," I said.

"Chambrun doesn't believe that?"

"He's asking for your help," I said.

Romy walked over to a desk in the corner of the room and sat down, pulling a pad of yellow legal paper toward him.

"Coffee?" Pam Smythe asked, indicating a percolator that was plugged into a wall socket under a side table.

"Thanks," I said. "You wouldn't have a piece of stale bread or an old sandwich somewhere? Breakfast seems to have gone by me."

Five minutes later I had coffee and a hearty ham sandwich. Romy was still scowling at his legal pad. Pam sat down beside me on the couch as I drank my coffee and ate my sandwich, grateful for both.

"It's a miserable world," Pam said. "People everywhere, on both sides of the political fence, want peace. The people in charge, the leaders, want power.

They try to persuade us that the only way to get the peace we want is to fight a war.''

"It's topsy-turvy time," I said.

"If there were no military secrets, no scientific or technological secrets, we could use what we know to make it a better world for everyone." She made an impatient gesture. "Even our love lives are tainted by this sick thinking. The fact that Romy is a gifted, talented, kind, witty man doesn't matter to my father. Romy is Russian, and all Russians are the enemy!"

"Give you a hard time?" I was already feeling better, thanks to the sandwich and coffee.

"As hard as he can. But, as I pointed out to you earlier, I'm over twenty-one! I live my life as I choose. Fortunately, I'm not dependent on Kenneth Smythe, the computer king, for my economic support. I had a grandfather named Bill Smith who left me enough to keep my head above water."

"Smith?"

She laughed a bitter little laugh. "When my father began to move in high places, 'Smith' became too commonplace for him. He changed his name to Smythe. I wonder how many of the names Romy will give you on his list are people's real names? I wonder how many of the facades we see are real and how many are fake? How many of the Smythes are Smiths? Romy is going to give you a list of people he thinks are two-faced. Could your Miss Ruysdale have been suckered by some two-faced charmer?"

"She has a man, a very solid love affair," I said.

"Could he be a double-dealer?"

"His name is Pierre Chambrun," I said.

She laughed. "Oh my! Well, I think my man is just as solid as you think her man is."

Romy was rising from the desk, a sheet of the yellow paper in his hand.

"I've only got eight names here for you, Mark," he said. "If I were asked for a list of all the people I know in the United States who might be agents of the KGB, it would take a book. But people who sometimes stay here at the Beaumont, or circulate regularly in the bars and restaurants, people Chambrun and Miss Ruysdale would know, boils down to eight. You probably know them yourself."

He handed me the paper, and I glanced at the list. There were two Russians who had some connection with that nation's United Nations delegation; a Brazilian businessman who throws rather lavish dinner parties from time to time; a Czech tennis player, a favorite of thousands of fans, who stays with us when the tennis action is here; a British actor who was at the moment starring in a play on Broadway (that one really surprised me); a West German businessman, in charge of the sale and distribution of a popular foreign-made car in the United States; a Greek shipping magnate who stayed with us about half of every year; and, finally, a Venezuelan gent, said to be raising funds for the rebels there, rebels with whom our government sympathizes. With the exception of the two Russians, they were all a surprise to me. I knew them all well enough to say hello to when I encountered them in the lobby or in one of the restaurants or bars. Good customers, all.

Pamela was smiling at me. "A collection of Smythe-Smiths," she said.

"I believe all of them are either staying here or have been in the hotel in the last forty-eight hours," Romy said. He sounded bitter when he went on. "Zachary's list will have at least one more name on it. Mine!"

Romy was right about Zachary's list in one respect. His name was on it. So was Pamela Smythe's. Guilt by association, I suppose. Also, Zachary's list involved about three dozen names. Air Force Intelligence evidently dug a lot deeper than Romy. It was also interesting that every one of Romy's eight names was also on Zachary's list.

Chambrun picked up on Pamela Smythe's name. "You actually think the Smythe girl belongs on this list?" he asked Zachary.

"She and Romanov travel everywhere together lately," Zachary said. "She provides him with an alibi for last night and this morning. But has it occurred to you, Chambrun, that he also supplies her with an alibi for the same time?"

"Slow process of checking out everyone on these lists," Lieutenant Hardy said. "Where were you from nine o'clock last night when the Willises disappeared until now? How many people will be as open about their night lives as Romanov and Miss Smythe?"

"The person or people we're looking for will have an alibi ready for us when we approach them," Zachary said. "That's why Romanov is at the top of my list, along with the Smythe girl. Romanov practically brought his alibi out into the hall to greet us when we first went to talk to him. He was too ready with an alibi. He had cultivated a friendship with Willis. Cocktails, a viewing of his paintings, an invitation to join them in the Blue Lagoon to hear that piano player. Romanov knew exactly where they'd be at a certain time. He meets them out in the hall as they are leaving for the Blue Lagoon. He's changed his mind, he'll go with them. They go to the elevator, operated by Tim Sullivan. Once in the elevator Romanov shows his true colors, produces a gun, orders Sullivan to take the elevator back up to seventeen, not down. Sullivan lunges at him and is shot dead for his pains. The elevator is taken up to where Miss Smythe is waiting. She takes care of the Willises, Romanov disposes of the man he's murdered. He lives here in the Beaumont. He probably knows the hotel as well as you do, Chambrun. He knew where that trash bin is in the basement."

"And where were the Willises held?" Hardy asked.

"Room 17E," Zachary said promptly. "Romanov was Henry Graves. Had the room ready at nine o'clock when the time came."

"Everyone in the hotel knows Romy," I said. "He couldn't have registered as Henry Graves without being recognized."

"A pair of dark glasses and a hat brim pulled down over his forehead would hide a multitude of sins," Zachary said. "Hell, man, we know Mrs. Willis was in 17E. That's where the brooch was found." He looked around at the others. "How much more do you need to get on the ball?"

"You want me to arrest him for murder?" Hardy asked.

"Of course not," Zachary said. "I want Romanov and the Smythe girl covered by the very best men you've got and Dodd has. I want you to turn the boy loose, Chambrun. I'll bet my next paycheck good old, kindly old, friend of the family Romanov or his girl-friend will pick up the boy, whisk him away, and take us straight to where the Willises are now being held. I want Willis rescued before he's forced to talk. What happens to Romanov after that is fun and games for you, Hardy."

"There's one thing you've left out," Hardy said. "Romanov knows you suspect him. If he is the man we're after, he'll be watching for just the kind of trap you're talking about."

"If he is working for the KGB," Chambrun said, "he won't lift a finger to pick up the boy, knowing how you feel about him, Zachary, and what you might set up to catch him. Turn the boy loose and he doesn't make a move. While we focus on him someone else on this list picks up the boy while Romanov laughs him-self sick over how stupid we are. We're not dealing with a homicidal maniac with a grudge, but with a massive spy system, highly paid, highly trained, highly patriotic, in all probability. We're dealing with a skilled army, not just one man. Right now the boy is the one weapon we have to keep Major Willis alive for a little longer. Guy stays in my place—unless you bring in the United States Army to take him away, Zach-ary."

Zachary raised his eyes to the ceiling as if he was looking for help from above. "So you're right. So it's not just one man we're after," he said. "But do you realize how vulnerable you are, Chambrun?"

"Vulnerable?"

"Stay stubborn, let your girlfriend go down the drain, and what's their next move to get their hands on the boy?"

"Tell me," Chambrun said.

"They blow up your precious hotel!" Zachary said. "Will you live a quiet old age knowing that your stubbornness has brought about the deaths of probably hundreds of people, the destruction of a massive business, and gained absolutely nothing? You won't let yourself be blackmailed, but I think you'll come to wish to God you'd never been born."

Chambrun was a stone statue.

"That's how they'd operate?" Hardy asked.

"Try to think sensibly for just one minute!" Zachary said. "What these people want from Willis is, they think, information that might save their nation from destruction by the enemy—the United States. Do you imagine they'd think twice about a few hundred people dead and a building destroyed? That boy might get them what they so desperately want. One stubborn man and his misjudgment of the situation isn't going to stand in their way." He waited for Chambrun to say something, but The Man stood rooted where he was, apparently thinking miles away from the moment. Zachary turned to me. "Where can I find a private phone? I'm going to get in touch with Washington, see if I can get to someone higher up who may persuade Chambrun to make sense."

I TOOK ZACHARY into Betsy's office. There was no one there, God help us. Zachary glared at the two phones on her desk.

"These both go through the switchboard?" he asked.

I told him the white phone was a direct line.

"I'd like privacy, if you don't mind," Zachary said.

I left him and went back to Chambrun and Hardy. The Man was sitting at his carved Florentine desk, drumming on its flat surface with the square, stubby fingers of his right hand. Hardy was standing over by the windows, watching Chambrun as if he expected something from him. I went over to the Turkish coffeemaker on the sideboard and brought Chambrun a cup of that vile-tasting brew he drank all day. It was Betsy who usually kept him supplied. He looked up at me as if he was surprised, and then muttered a thanks.

Chambrun sipped the coffee and lit one of the flat Egyptian cigarettes he smokes. He exhaled smoke in a long sigh. "To answer a question that has no answers," he said.

"The question of what to do in case—?" Hardy asked.

Chambrun nodded. "I'm not a member of Zachary's fan club," he said, "but the man works in the world of spies and secret agents every day of his life. How that kind of person might act in a given situation is kindergarten stuff to him. Bomb a great hotel filled with hundreds of famous people is unthinkable to us. It's the first thing that comes to Zachary's mind."

"Why not? It's everywhere, Pierre," Hardy said. "They bomb a hotel in England where the lady Prime Minister is staying; they bomb American military installations in West Germany; they bomb everything in sight in Beirut; they bomb embassies and railroad stations and buses and airplanes. You can find a bombing in every day's paper and hear about them on radio and TV. Bombs are the tools of terrorists everywhere. Zachary doesn't have to be a genius to have thought of a bombing."

"I guess I was suffering from the great American delusion," Chambrun said. "I won't be mugged or robbed or raped, not me! It will only happen to the other guy. My hotel won't be bombed—not my hotel. It may happen in London or Liverpool or Beirut, but not here in my hotel."

"Don't cross that bridge until you have to," Hardy said.

"Zachary knows how they think," Chambrun said. "It could happen, and it wouldn't be aimed at the corporation that owns the hotel, or any of the hundreds of guests, or just to create an incident of terror. It would be aimed straight at me, to force me to turn an eleven-year-old boy over to a gang of butchers!"

"So it hasn't happened yet," Hardy said. "They'll have to threaten you before they act."

"But what do you do if they make the threat?" I asked Chambrun.

Chambrun made a strange little gesture with his hands, like a juggler throwing three or four balls in the air. "You're right to ask, Mark," he said. "There are several choices, but I have to decide before the threat comes which one I'm going to make, don't I?"

"The first one being that you let them have the boy," Hardy said.

"Unacceptable," Chambrun said sharply.

"Boy rates above Betsy Ruysdale, above hundreds of your guests, above the hotel itself and God knows how many of your people?" Hardy asked.

"The boy isn't just a gambling chip, Walter," Chambrun said. "Let him go and we let him die, let his father and mother die, and convey important military secrets to the enemy. None of the Willises will live after the Major is persuaded to talk to save his boy. They already know too much about who the enemy is and who is giving the orders. So would Betsy."

"So you sit tight and let them hit you where you live?"

Chambrun crushed out his cigarette in the desk ashtray.

"So we batten down the hatches and wait it out," he said.

"Or we tell the guests now that there's been a bomb threat, empty the hotel, and wait for their next move."

"Moving the boy to where?" Hardy said.

"No matter what the choice, I'm not leaving the Beaumont," Chambrun said. "I think a large majority of the people who work for me will stand by. Emptied of customers, it's going to be hard for someone to march in here and plant a bomb."

"Cost you hundreds of thousands of dollars in business," Hardy said.

"And save scores of lives. That's a choice I can make without difficulty. Can we get the police bomb squad here, Walter?"

Harry nodded and reached for the phone. Chambrun turned to me. "Get Jerry. There's been a bomb threat. Restaurants and bars to be evacuated and closed, shops closed, registered guests gotten out. Staff are asked to stand by, but are free to go."

"But there hasn't been a threat yet!"

"We don't know that a bomb hasn't already been planted, ready to be triggered when they choose," Chambrun said. "If it hasn't been, maybe we can prevent it from happening. Get moving, Mark."

IT MAY NOT BE a surprise to anyone who knows the Beaumont or has read any of the stories that have been written about Pierre Chambrun that a routine for instant evacuation of the hotel had been long ago established. In the days of the war in Vietnam, most large metropolises with their large railroad stations, airports, hotels, hospitals, and the like had set up evacuation procedures to guard against the possibility of bombs being dropped by missiles or airplanes as an act of war. We had been through that evacuation drill dozens of times at the Beaumont. Everyone knew exactly where to go and what do do.

Five minutes after Chambrun gave the order it was under way over the telephone switchboard, over loudspeakers, and special warnings given by key people who knew exactly how to spread the word. There was something special added to the order this time.

"This is NOT a drill! This is NOT a drill!"

My particular assignment in the procedure was to deal with the press. On this particular morning we were flooded with them, already dealing with three major stories—the murder of Tim Sullivan, the abduction of Major Willis and his wife, and the kidnapping of Betsy Ruysdale used as a weapon to force Chambrun to release the Willis boy.

A loudspeaker in the lobby informed reporters that there would be an announcement for them in the ballroom at the rear of the lobby.

"It is a bomb threat, we assume from the people responsible for the disappearances of Major Willis and his wife and Miss Ruysdale," I told the mob of press, television, and radio reporters who flocked there. "The hotel is being emptied so that the police bomb squad can work more efficiently."

"Will Chambrun give up the boy?" a dozen voices shouted at me.

"An answer to that question might place key people in danger," I told them. "The main thing now is to get out of here before something blows you out! I'll be back here as soon as the bomb squad says the coast is clear."

"Today or next week?" a sour voice asked.

"When they tell us it's safe, not before," I said. "Now, move please!"

I had seen and been a part of evacuation drills before. People left, laughing and joking, the registered guests leaving their belongings in their rooms because they knew it was only a drill. This morning there was little or no laughing and joking. "This is NOT a drill!" There were no bellboys to help them, and people carried hastily packed bags and briefcases themselves. There was almost no hysteria that I could see. Most of the in-house guests must already have heard on TV or radio what had been going on in the hotel since early morning. It wasn't a total surprise to hear of a bomb threat. Cooperation was the name of the game. There was little or no casual street business in the restaurants at that hour of the morning—just after nine o'clock. Too late for breakfast, too early for lunch. The bars don't open until ten o'clock, so there was no problem of getting merrymakers to leave. I didn't take the time to look, but the streets outside the Beaumont must have been bedlam, hundreds of people blocking traffic to wait and watch.

I went back up to Chambrun's office, where he was holding a telephone, obviously getting a running report from someone.

"Clockwork," I told him.

He just nodded and went on making notes on the report he was getting. The door to his office burst open and Captain Zachary charged in. Chambrun's face hardened and he put down the phone, after telling someone he'd call back in a few minutes.

"You got the threat?" Zachary asked.

"That's the story," Chambrun said.

"They threatened to blow up your hotel?"

"You told me they would," Chambrun said. "I decided not to wait for it."

"So all this clearing out is a fake?"

"It's real enough," Chambrun said. "When we've emptied out the guests, the police bomb squad will find out if a bomb has been planted. If they don't find one, they'll make sure one isn't planted in the future."

"The Willis boy being taken out, too?" Zachary asked.

"You know the tradition, Zachary. The captain never leaves his sinking ship. If the Beaumont is to go down, I'll go with it. And the boy stays with me, suffers the same fate I do."

"In your penthouse?"

"If I decide that's the safest place," Chambrun said.

Zachary's face was dark with anger. "Do you think you have the right, Chambrun, to decide how this Willis case should be handled? Do you think you have the right to decide not to let the Willis boy go when that might lead us to where Major Willis is being held and keep vital information from the enemy?"

"I have the same right to decide what goes on in this hotel as any head of the family does in his own home."

"I've just finished talking to my boss in Washington," Zachary said. "Colonel Martin is prepared to get a court order forcing you to turn the boy over to us—if I can't persuade you to do it voluntarily."

"You can tell your Colonel Martin that he'd better send in the marines if he wants to serve me with a court order. I have an obligation to protect that boy, Zachary, and I will follow my own judgment on the best way to do it."

"Endangering the whole damn country in the process?"

"I happen to think that keeping the boy safe may be the best way of keeping Major Willis's secrets safe.

You can tell your Colonel Martin I'm on this end of the phone if he wants to talk to me."

Without Betsy Ruysdale in her outer office, the entrance to Chambrun's office was like a revolving door. People could come and go at will. Jerry Dodd, our security chief, came in walking another man ahead of him. The man was vaguely familiar, but I could not place him for a moment. He was medium tall with brown hair, cut short, and an amiable smile on his face.

"I thought you and Captain Zachary might want to talk to this man," Jerry said. "Mr. Cardoza was at his post in the lobby when he spotted Father Callahan wandering around and told me."

The gun-toting priest! Without his turnaround collar, I hadn't placed him. I saw Chambrun pat at his left shoulder.

"All clean this trip," Jerry said. "No gun."

"A joke, is a joke, is a joke," the man I knew as Father Callahan said. "Would someone mind telling me what the hell this is all about? I am practically placed under arrest by this man and brought up here against my will. Speaking of guns, does he have a license for the one he stuck in my ribs?"

"He does," Chambrun said. "You are Father Paul Callahan?"

"I certainly am not," the man said.

"Then who are you?" Chambrun asked.

The man's smile broadened. "I was christened Francisco Garibaldi," he said. "That was almost fifty years ago. My family came to this country from Italy about then. Italians weren't very popular here in those days, thanks to Benito Mussolini. My father changed his name from Anthony Garibaldi to Tony Gary. I became Frank Gary. My mother, Serefina, became Sarah Gary. You want to see my citizenship papers?''

"Mark?'' Chambrun asked, looking at me.

"At around one-thirty or a quarter of two this morning,'' I said, "this man, wearing a priest's collar and calling himself Father Paul Callahan, was in the Blue Lagoon trying to persuade young Guy Willis to leave the hotel with him.''

"No question about that, according to Cardoza,'' Jerry said.

"How do you account for that, Mr. Gary—if that's your name?''

"He is carrying a driver's license with his photograph on it,'' Jerry Dodd said. "Name of Frank Gary.''

"A chauffeur's license, if you want to be exact,'' the man said. "I own and operate a limousine service. You'll find me listed in the Yellow Pages. I have to be licensed to operate my own cars in case I find myself short a driver.''

"You weren't here in the Blue Lagoon between one-thirty and two this morning?''

"What is the Blue Lagoon? In any case, my wife can tell you I was at home in bed, sound asleep at that time.''

"Another bedroom alibi,'' Zachary muttered, obviously thinking of Romy Romanov, his pet suspect.

"What are you doing here in the hotel this morning?'' Chambrun asked.

"I guess you could say 'Curiosity killed the cat,'" the man said. "Over my breakfast coffee I heard a radio account of what was going on here. Driving to work I pass by here, and curiosity got the best of me. I thought I'd drop in and see what the excitement was all about. I was wandering around the lobby when this big Spanish-looking guy grabbed me and shouted for Dodd here. I was arrested—without a warrant, by the way—unceremoniously searched for a weapon, and brought up here. Now, can we call it quits and let me out of here before your hotel blows up?"

"There's the waiter who served him in the Blue Lagoon," Chambrun said to Jerry. "There's Waters, the doorman who saw a priest leaving the hotel a little after two in the morning. If they also identify this man as Father Callahan—"

"There's the boy," Zachary said. "He sat eye-to-eye with the priest at a table in the nightclub, I was told. He wrestled with him and felt the gun he was carrying in a shoulder holster. Bring the boy down here, Chambrun, and we can stop guessing."

"The boy stays put," Chambrun said. "We'll take Mr. Gary up to my penthouse."

"You can't keep dragging me around places!" Gary said.

"In a criminal crisis in this hotel," Chambrun said, "I am the law."

One elevator in the left bank had been reserved for hotel use, operating on a self-service basis. Five of us—Chambrun, Jerry Dodd, Zachary, the man who called himself Gary, and I—took it to the roof, passing by the checkpoint at the thirty-ninth floor where

Chambrun gave the secret code words that let us go on up to the roof.

I have to take time out for a minute to reintroduce Victoria Haven to Chambrun's followers. She is an astonishing old girl, with her scarlet hair, elegant figure, her still-handsome if wrinkled face. She was there with Guy Willis when we arrived, and it looked as if he'd finally met his match at gin rummy. The poker chips being used for money were mostly stacked on her side of the table. Victoria's gentleman friend, the little Japanese spaniel, greeted us with angry barks. He tolerates Chambrun and Jerry and me, announcing our presence on the roof with a few sharp shrieks when we come alone. But Zachary and the man who called himself Gary were strangers, and his outrage was endless until the old lady picked him up by the scruff of his neck and held him in her lap. He sat there, teeth bared, daring the enemy to come closer.

The boy's reaction was instant. He sprang off his chair and ran to Chambrun, his face working.

"That's the priest with the gun," he said. "He's the one in my nightmare, beating my parents!"

Gary shook his head. "I'm part of a bad dream?"

"Interesting, wouldn't you say, Mr. Gary?" Chambrun said. "How could the boy get you into a dream if he hadn't seen you somewhere before? He couldn't invent you, could he?"

"I think it's time I got some kind of legal help," Gary said. "Am I entitled to that one phone call?"

Chambrun was the hanging judge again. "You can make a phone call," he said. "But it will be a little complicated for your lawyer to get to you. No one will be admitted in off the street while this bomb scare is on, and I don't think you'll be allowed to go to him."

"You'll prevent it?" Gary asked. He wasn't amused any longer.

Chambrun turned to Jerry Dodd. "See if you can locate Lieutenant Hardy and get him up here, Jerry." Then, back to Gary, "The abduction of the Willises is connected with a murder—one of the elevator operators. You, in your role as Father Callahan, were obviously involved in trying to get the boy away from here, an act connected to that crime. Homicide may very well want to hold you as an accessory to a killing."

"How many times do I have to tell you that I am not 'Father Callahan,' nor did I ever pretend to be?"

"So far we have three witnesses who say you are or pretended to be a priest, and I may be able to produce two more," Chambrun said. "Whatever your game is, you've lost it, Gary. Why not decide to make a deal for yourself, possibly immunity, by telling the truth?"

Zachary turned impatiently away from the window where he'd been standing, listening. "You know a man named Alexander Romanov?" he asked Gary.

"Never heard of him. Who is he?"

"He's a Russian portrait painter who is probably right in the center of all this mess," Zachary said. "Were you working with him? Were you trying to get the boy away so that Romanov could use him to force his father to spill what he knows?"

"All of you should be collaborating on a television soap opera," Gary said. "I've never heard of your Russian painter. I never laid eyes on this boy until you brought me up here just now, no matter what he says, no matter what his dreams are.''

"Once more, Mark," Chambrun said to me.

"This is the man I saw in the Blue Lagoon with Guy early this morning. He introduced himself to me as 'Father Callahan.' He said he'd been a chaplain in the Air Force in Vietnam and that Major Willis was an old friend from war days. He'd stopped in at the Blue Lagoon to hear Duke Hines play the piano. By chance he heard Guy report to Mr. Cardoza that his parents were missing. He said he wanted to take the boy under his wing as a favor to an old friend."

"He tried to drag me away," the boy said, "and I could feel the gun he was wearing in a shoulder holster."

Gary shook his head. "I've heard of freak cases where there were two people, unconnected or related, who looked exactly alike. That must be what's happened here."

"Same voice. Same speech pattern," I said. There was absolutely no doubt in my mind.

There was a moment of silence, and then Jerry Dodd spoke to Chambrun. "I'd better get back to what's going on downstairs, Boss. What do you want done with this character?"

You could almost hear Chambrun's brain clicking as he worked on a decision. "Penthouse Number Three is unoccupied," he said finally. Number Three was reserved for special U.N. big shots, and I happened to know it was being held for some British dignitaries due to arrive the following day. "Take Mr. Gary over there and lock him in," Chambrun went on.

"When I have time, I'll visit you, Gary, and let you know exactly what your situation is."

"My situation is fairly obvious," Gary said. "I'm being illegally held prisoner. That is going to cost you the biggest lawsuit you ever heard of, Chambrun. Do I use that phone to make my one call?"

"I've changed my mind about that," Chambrun said. "There'll be no outgoing calls while this crisis persists."

"And when you find there isn't any bomb?"

"The bomb isn't the crisis I'm talking about," Chambrun said. His voice was scary cold. "A friend of mine and his wife are being held prisoner, probably worked over, threatened, tortured. The most precious lady in my life is in the same boat. I think you know where they are, Gary. 'Father Callahan' was supposed to take the boy to his parents, wasn't he? So, when you decide to tell me where they are, and if we find them safe and in one piece, I may turn you loose to bring your lawsuit. If you don't tell us and we don't find them, you'll never get to bring your lawsuit, friend. I make you a promise. You will die in the most painful way I can possibly devise for you." He turned to Jerry. "Take him away. Lock him in Penthouse Three. Notify the switchboard that there are to be no outgoing calls from Penthouse Three. And if anyone calls or comes and asks for Mr. Gary, you never heard of him. If they ask for Father Callahan, get them to me."

"You have just arranged for your own destruction when I get out of this," Gary said.

"You arranged for your own destruction when you walked into this hotel and involved yourself with the Willises," Chambrun said. "You have an out, though. You can talk."

Gary turned to Jerry Dodd and held out his arms as though he expected to be handcuffed. The little dog in Victoria Haven's lap snarled angrily as Jerry took his prisoner away.

"OF COURSE, he knows you're bluffing," Zachary said when Jerry had taken his man away.

"Then he's living in a fool's paradise," Chambrun said. "There isn't an ounce of bluff in anything I told him."

"You'd actually think of killing him?"

"If Miss Ruysdale isn't returned to me unharmed, I wouldn't have anything to live for," Chambrun said. "I couldn't wait to get at him."

If anyone but Chambrun had made such a threat, I'd probably have thought it was just big talk. Knowing him, I was almost certain he meant it.

"Are you going to just camp here on Romy Romanov's trail," Chambrun asked the Air Force man, "or are you going to check out all the people on your list of suspects and the one Romy gave us? You and your intelligence people could be useful if you weren't determined to take an easy way out. Have you decided Gary is telling the truth? That would make it simpler for you, wouldn't it?"

Zachary was struggling to keep his anger from flaring up again. "I think Gary is a liar," he said. "Haskell here and the boy make it pretty certain. He was

'Father Callahan.' But where does that get us? He's a tough cookie. He isn't going to talk, threats or no threats. So, he's part of a team working for the enemy. Romanov is probably part of that same team. Major Willis could never have been suckered into a trap by anyone but a friend. Romanov was such a friend. Romanov actually knew Willis and his wife were going down to the Blue Lagoon. He'd been invited to go with them. He was ready for them when the time came."

"So?"

"So my next move is to try to find someone who has been in contact with both Romanov and Gary during the last few days. That would take us a step closer to the main man, whoever he is."

"And meanwhile, what happens to Betsy Ruysdale and the Willises? Can we wait for that kind of investigation? It could take days."

"I keep telling you," Zachary said, his voice rising, "turn the boy loose. Someone will pick him up and they'll lead us to the people you want to save."

Guy Willis faced Chambrun. "I'm not afraid, if it would do it, Mr. Chambrun. You say you don't want to live if Betsy isn't all right. Well, I don't want to live if my parents aren't all right."

"So we let them use you to force your father to talk," Chambrun said. "And, when he has talked, you will all be dead because your father and mother, and Betsy, can expose them. The one hope I can see for keeping them alive, boy, is not to let you be used to make them talk. If Captain Zachary would get off his butt we just might find another lead to them without involving you. You, here and safe, are the one card we have to play to keep the people we love alive for a little longer. For God's sake, Zachary, get sensible!''

Zachary swore softly under his breath, turned away, and walked out of the penthouse. Toto, the Japanese gentleman friend, snarled angrily as he left.

"Not a nice man," Victoria Haven said. She put the dog down, went to the terrace door, and let her friend out onto the roof. "Has to do his duty. His instinct about people is seldom wrong."

Chambrun didn't comment, might actually not have heard. He was reaching out in his mind for something, something he thought ought to be there and that he couldn't quite locate.

"I believe you really would kill that Gary man, Pierre," Victoria said.

"When we have lost. But we haven't lost yet," Chambrun said.

"This whole drama has been staged here in the Beaumont," the old lady said. "Zachary is right, you know. Major Willis could only have been lured into a trap by a friend, or at least someone he trusted." She looked down at the boy, who seemed more tense than I'd seen him, even when he was being threatened by 'Father Callahan.' "Maybe Guy could tell us what other friends his father had staying here in the hotel?"

Guy's lips trembled when he spoke. "I think I told Mr. Chambrun that Mr. Romanov had been a friend from back before I was born. My dad was stationed in Moscow. They knew each other there—before I was ever born."

"Have you stayed here with your parents before, Guy?" Victoria asked him. "On other trips to New York?"

"No," Chambrun said, sounding abstracted.

"I've only been to New York with them twice before, when I was quite small. We stayed somewhere else, a big hotel that faces the south end of the Park."

"The Plaza," Chambrun said in that small faraway voice.

"Yes, that was it," the boy said. "Rozzie took me for rides in a hansom cab—you know, a horse cab?"

"I know," Victoria said. "Believe it or not, Guy, I can remember when that was the way to get around in cities—London, New York, Paris." She smiled. "I can remember some romantic encounters in hansom cabs."

"You're straying from the subject at hand, Victoria," Chambrun said. "My encounter with Ham Willis was just over two years ago. He'd come here to the Beaumont for a meeting with someone from one of the U.N. delegations. I had gone out to the bank on business. On my way home I was attacked by muggers just down the block. Ham Willis luckily, was just leaving the hotel. He was armed, and he was a brave man. He almost certainly saved my life. We became friends. After that, when he came to New York he made the Beaumont his base of operations. But Guy can't tell you anything about his connections here except for this visit, which began three days ago."

"Mr. Romanov was the only friend you met?" Victoria asked the boy.

"There was a Miss Smythe who was with Mr. Romanov," the boy said, "but I don't think Dad and Rozzie had met her before."

"Your father didn't mention any other friends in your presence who might be staying here?"

The boy shook his head. "Just Mr. Chambrun, who I was to trust and feel free to call on if I was in any trouble."

"So he had no friend staying here in the hotel," Victoria said.

"That doesn't mean a friend wasn't circulating here—without being a guest," Chambrun said.

"You don't want to face it, do you, Pierre?" the lady said.

I didn't know what she was talking about, but he did. He made an impatient gesture, as though he was brushing away an irritating fly.

Victoria looked at me. "Vanity isn't a good crutch to lean on when important friends are in trouble," she said.

"Vanity?" I didn't know what she was talking about.

"Pierre prides himself on his judgments of people," the lady said. Perhaps I should mention here that I've heard rumors around the hotel that once upon a time there had been a young man-older woman thing between Chambrun and Mrs. Haven. She, at least, knew him rather more intimately than most of us who had come to work here long after Victoria and Chambrun had been good neighbors on the hotel rooftop. "But a hundred percent right would be a miracle, wouldn't it?"

"Say whatever it is you have on your mind and get it over with, Vicky," Chambrun said. "This day is just racing past us, and we have no time."

"So be it, Pierre. You seem to accept the idea that Major Willis was led into a trap by a friend or someone he trusted. So he had no friends here but you, and you didn't lead him into a trap. But this is your hotel; he has every reason to trust you and the people you trust, Pierre—your staff. There is someone here he's gotten to know over the last couple of years, someone who's made a point of serving him well. Someone in whom you've misplaced your faith, Pierre; someone who has betrayed you and Major Willis, and worst of all, Betsy!"

"That's just not possible," Chambrun said. As I've mentioned, the Boss is an extraordinary man about the hundreds of people who work in the hotel. He knows about their private lives, their spouses, their children, their outside interests. No one would last very long with him who didn't merit his trust, certainly not the two years that Major Willis had been coming to the Beaumont.

"It may not be," Victoria said, "but surely, Pierre, it's possible. As I understand it, there could be huge sums of money involved—bribes that would almost certainly turn some heads. It's possible, Pierre, and you should examine that possibility. Who, in the two years Major Willis has been coming here, has paid him particular attention, provided him with special services? A room-service waiter, a bellboy or bell captain, a desk clerk, someone who handles the theater-ticket agency, a valet. It could be anyone, Pierre, not necessarily someone in an important position. I would give my arm for the room-service maid who takes care of me every day. If I found a diamond ring missing I'd know she wasn't the thief, couldn't be. And yet she might be. You have to consider, Pierre, that someone you trust may not be trustworthy."

He sat silent for a few moments, scowling at the expanse of blue sky that was visible through the windows. Then he turned to the lady and touched her hand with a little gesture of affection. "Thanks, Vicky, for not letting me fall asleep at the switch," he said.

TWO

"IT ISN'T PLEASANT to have your weaknesses pointed out to you in public," Chambrun said. He and I were alone in that self-service elevator descending from the roof to the lobby.

"I don't think of myself as the 'public,'" I said, "and surely it can't be so bad to have a good friend like Mrs. Haven make a suggestion to you."

"'Vanity,'" he said. "I don't think of myself as vain, but I am proud of this hotel. I am proud of the fact that in more than twenty years not a single employee I've hired to work here has turned sour on me. Pride and vanity are not quite the same, do you think?"

"I would never have used the word 'vanity' in connection with you, Boss," I said. "But there are unusual factors involved here. Money, for instance. Enough money could be offered to turn an honest man a little dizzy."

"There isn't a single man or woman working in the Beaumont who doesn't know that if they found themselves in trouble they could come to me for help."

"But would you give them a million bucks to handle as they chose?"

He gave me a cold look. "Would you sell three or four human lives for a million dollars, Mark?"

I tried to keep it light. "I might think about it for about ten seconds," I said.

He gave me the faintest of smiles. "Ten seconds is far longer than an honest man would need," he said. "Maybe, when this is over, we should have a talk about it. I may have misjudged you, Mark."

I was grateful for the smile. He had to be kidding.

He stopped the elevator at the second floor, but he had orders for me. "Find Johnny Thacker and Mike Maggio for me," he said. "Jerry, when he can get free, and Mrs. Kniffin, who is the housekeeper on the seventeenth floor. Hardy, if you see him." He left the elevator and went down the corridor to his office.

Johnny Thacker and Mike Maggio are the day and night bell captains at the Beaumont, trusted employees at the top level. Mike would normally be off duty and at home at this time of day, but he almost certainly wouldn't have left the hotel with all that was brewing today.

I don't know if I can properly describe what the lobby was like when I got there. It was like a stage set with the actors gone somewhere to take a break. There were one or two strangers who didn't belong there, policemen with dogs! They use those beautiful German shepherds to sniff for bombs as well as drugs. There was no one at the front desk, but I caught a glimpse of Atterbury, the head day clerk, moving in the small office back of the desk. The evacuation had obviously gone well. There weren't even any stragglers. Two of Jerry's men were stationed at the main entrance, obviously to keep anyone from coming in from the street. Beyond those doors I could hear the sound of hundreds of voices, rising and falling like waves on a beach. I felt, suddenly, as though I were in a strange place. And then I saw Mike Maggio, the night bell captain, emerging from the rear corridor that leads to the private dining rooms and the grand ballroom.

Mike is Italian, as his name suggests, dark-haired with bright black eyes and an almost perpetual professional smile. He grew up a smart street kid, and he's about as quick as anyone I know to spot a phony, or someone who doesn't have the best interests of the Beaumont on his mind. Jerry Dodd has asked more than once to have Mike transferred to his security force, but Chambrun felt he could serve the hotel better in a position that didn't attract attention to him as "the law."

"Rats have all deserted the sinking ship," Mike said as he walked up to me.

"The boss wants you in his office," I told him. "Also Johnny, Jerry if he can get untracked, and Lieutenant Hardy if you can find him."

"Just saw him," Mike said. "He's down in the basement where they found Tim Sullivan. All kinds of cops standing around playing guessing games. What the hell's going on, Mark? Anything on Betsy?"

"Nothing. But the boss will bring you up to date. I've got to try to locate Mrs. Kniffin."

"Telephone," Mike said. "Not even bombs or earthquakes can move old Kate out of her linen room on seventeen. I'll round up Johnny and the others for you."

"The Boss isn't a patient man today," I said.

"I can imagine," Mike said, taking off. Then he stopped and called back to me. "If I don't get a chance, tell The Man he can count on me to help break some arms and legs over Betsy."

MRS. KNIFFIN, the motherly old housekeeper who had been at the Beaumont almost as long as Chambrun himself, was exactly where Mike said she would be, in her linen room on seventeen. I waited for her in the lobby and we went up to Chambrun's office together.

"Like a ghost town," she said as we went upstairs.

Mike Maggio had taken me at my word, and he and Johnny Thacker were already there when Mrs. Kniffin and I arrived. Jerry Dodd and Lieutenant Hardy had been notified and would come as soon as they could get free.

"We don't know any more than we did hours ago about where Major Willis and his wife are, or Betsy," Chambrun told them. "But there are ways you three might help."

"Name it," Johnny Thacker said. He is the direct opposite of Mike Maggio in appearance—flaxen blond hair, blue eyes, tall and slender.

"We think it's certain," Chambrun told them, "that Major Willis and his wife were tricked by someone they thought was a friend or someone they trusted. We think it's certain Betsy let someone she knew and trusted into her apartment, was roughed up and taken away. That suggests someone in the hotel who knew both the Willises and Betsy."

"That Air Force character thinks it's Mr. Romanov," Mike said. "He's asked me a thousand questions about him."

"Miss Smythe gives him an alibi," Chambrun said.

"He's her guy. She would," Johnny said.

"But Betsy wouldn't invite him up to her apartment at four o'clock in the morning," Chambrun said. "Not the way things are."

"Romanov is your friend," Mike said. "If he told Betsy he had a message from you—"

"I would have phoned her. She already knew what Zachary thought about Romy. She wouldn't have opened the gate for him."

"So who are you aiming at?" Mike asked.

Chambrun explained his theory of the enormous bribe. Johnny Thacker bristled.

"You think maybe one of us—?"

"Don't be a damn fool, Johnny," Mike Maggio said. "If he thought that, he'd have us hangin' out to dry somewhere, not here in his office, talking."

Chambrun ignored that byplay. "Even the boy can't tell us too much about his father's friends," he said. "Ham Willis fought a war in Vietnam, West Point and the Air Force before that, diplomatic posts in Central America, Europe, Russia. He knows people all around the world, many of whom he'd trust."

"No way to guess," Mike said.

"Betsy Ruysdale is another story," Chambrun said.

"In what way?" Mike asked. "She's worked here in the hotel for—how long—ten years?"

"Twelve," Chambrun said.

"In that time tens of thousands of people have passed through the place. The number of people she knows could make Major Willis look like a piker. She not only knows them, she knows about them, thanks to your files on registered guests—their financial status, their sex habits, how they handle alcohol and drugs. It would scare the hell out of most of our guests if they knew how much we know about them. Pretty hard to guess who Betsy might trust, wouldn't you say?"

"No, I wouldn't," Chambrun said. "Let's not play it cute right now, Mike. I know Betsy, how she thinks, how her mind works, better than anyone else in the world. I can tell you that, not counting me, there aren't more than three people Betsy would have let up to her room at four o'clock this morning. Nothing had happened to alert the Willises at nine o'clock last night, but at four o'clock this morning we had a kidnapping and a murder. Betsy would have been on guard."

"And the three people, she'd have let up to her apartment—not counting you?" Mike asked.

"Jerry Dodd, you, and Johnny," Chambrun said. "I should add Mark to that list, but I happen to know exactly where he was at that time. In my penthouse with the Willis boy."

"So one of us has sold you out," Johnny Thacker said in a tight, hard voice.

"That has never occurred to me for a moment," Chambrun said. "I ought to know another person she would trust that much, and I don't."

"Someone Betsy trusted and the Willises too," Johnny said. "Someone like Romanov."

"Not necessarily," Chambrun said. "We're working against a whole system of agents for another country. It doesn't have to be just one person who trapped the Willises and also struck at Betsy."

"If she was picked up on the street before she ever got home—" Johnny said.

"She wasn't. Someone other than Betsy was in that apartment, remade the bed. Someone had to let that person in."

"Her keys, taken from her when she was picked up," Johnny said.

"Then why remake the bed if it didn't need it?" Chambrun asked.

No one seemed to know where to go from there for a moment. I should have guessed it would be Mike who'd come up with an idea.

"If I was in Betsy's position," Mike said, "warned of danger, there is one person I might trust, unlock doors for, who I didn't know at all."

"In your right mind?" Johnny asked.

"Of course. I might trust a cop. Look, the place here was crawling with cops. Somebody rings Betsy's front-door buzzer, says he's one of Hardy's men. The Lieutenant needs answers to some questions about hotel routines. He tells her Mr. Chambrun is occupied and she is the most likely person to have answers he needs."

"Betsy might buy that," Chambrun agreed.

"So she springs the front door for him," Mike said, "he comes upstairs and she opens her apartment door for him."

"And he isn't a cop," Johnny said.

"He isn't wearing a blue suit, if that's what you mean. But he has a badge and the regular ID. Plainclothesmen are everywhere in the hotel right this minute. A million-dollar operation, police badges could come their way in bags, like potato chips . . ."

"So one of Hardy's men has been bought by the other side," Johnny said.

"Maybe you didn't get enough sleep, dummy!" Mike said. "I didn't say he was one of Hardy's men. I said he said he was one of Hardy's men. That would explain why Betsy'd let a stranger into her place at that time, wouldn't it, Boss?"

Chambrun nodded, slowly. "It could be," he said. "And that means we don't have to be looking for some friend of Betsy's, just an actor pretending to be a plainclothesman."

Mike grinned, pleased with himself. "You don't have to be an actor to pretend to be a cop. Just don't look too bright!"

None of us laughed at his joke. We were imagining a strange man, faking his way into Betsy's apartment, roughing her up, dragging her out of there against her will.

"He could have had a confederate downstairs, waiting with a car," Johnny said. "She didn't call for help. Jerry questioned other tenants in the building."

"She couldn't call for help if she'd been gagged, or knocked unconscious. No one around the hallways at four A.M. No people on the street," Mike said.

"I don't like to buy it," Chambrun said after a moment.

"Why not, Boss?" Mike asked.

"It explains how it could have happened, but it leaves us with no leads at all."

"Fingerprints," Mike said. "If this guy remade Betsy's bed and straightened up the apartment, he must have left prints."

"What's this about fingerprints?" a voice asked from behind us. Lieutenant Hardy had joined us.

Chambrun explained Mike's theory about the fake cop.

"Ingenious," Hardy said, "and quite possible. We're involved in an ugly game here, so much money available you have to know your own mother might sell you out. We dusted that apartment for prints, Pierre, and came up with a hat full. Thanks to your security system here at the Beaumont, every employee is fingerprinted and those prints kept on file. We know, of course, that Betsy was in her apartment, there were some prints of yours, Pierre, and a couple belonging to a hotel maid named Nancy Coughlin who is moonlighting as a cleaning woman for Betsy. Then there are one or two more."

"Who?" Mike asked, eager to have his theory prove out.

"There's an unfortunate thing about fingerprints, Mike," Hardy said. "They don't have a name on them. They're no use to you unless you can match them with someone's. So what do we match those other prints against? We don't even have a suspect. They might help to hang a man someday—after we've caught him.''

''Romanov and his lady friend,'' Mike suggested.

''I have a feeling that would just add another rivet to his alibi,'' Chambrun said.

''You still don't buy him as a suspect, Pierre?'' Hardy asked.

''Gut feeling,'' Chambrun said.

''Who don't you have a gut feeling about, Boss?'' Mike asked.

''The whole damned world out there,'' Chambrun said.

''I'm afraid we're going to find that's where we are—out there,'' Hardy said. ''The theory that the Willises and Betsy are being held somewhere in the hotel, moved around as we search places and don't think we have to go back to them, is beginning to run out of gas. All the paying customers are off the grounds now. The police, Jerry's men, the bomb squad with dogs, are going over the place, inch by inch. A bomb wouldn't have to be any bigger than a grapefruit. When that search is over and we haven't found Betsy and the Willises, we have to know that they are being held 'out there' somewhere.''

''If they are still being held,'' Chambrun said, his voice grim.

''I have a 'gut feeling' about that,'' Hardy said. ''What these people want from Major Willis is so important to them they just won't throw him away, or anyone who can be used to make him talk. It didn't work with his wife, so we have to write a question mark after her name. Betsy wasn't expected to get him to talk. She was to force you to release the boy who could be used to break down his father.''

"And that hasn't worked so far.''

"I don't mean to scare you, Pierre, but I have a feeling you will hear again, some evidence that Betsy's in big trouble.''

"Evidence?''

"It's happened before, Pierre. An ear, a finger—a photograph showing her in some unbearable situation.''

"Oh my God!'' Chambrun muttered.

"I happen to agree with you,'' Hardy said. "Turn the boy loose and they snatch him. Torturing the kid in front of his father may get what they want. After that, good-bye Willises and good-bye Betsy. They will know too much.''

"So what do I do? Just wait here for the bad news to come?'' Chambrun sounded almost desperate.

"I've been talking to Colonel Martin, Willis's commanding officer in Washington,'' Hardy said. "Zachary has been trying to persuade him to get a court order to force you to release the boy. I've persuaded him to come up here and talk with you and the boy and Zachary before he takes any such action. He's cn his way. He should be here in a couple of hours. Meanwhile—''

Chambrun's phone blinked its little red light at us and he picked it up and answered. Then, "Put her on, Mrs. Veach.'' He reached out and threw the switch on the squawk box that would make the phone conversation audible to all of us. "Mrs. Haven," he said. "Some emergency about the boy?"

"Pierre?" The old lady's voice came over the box. "What's wrong, Vicky?"

"I seem to have lost my ability to charm young men," Mrs. Haven said with a kind of chuckle. I had the feeling she was putting on a performance for someone who was there with her. "Your young card-sharp decided he'd had enough of my company. Went to the bathroom, slipped out the window there onto the roof, and tried to take off down the fire stairs. Fortunately, Jerry Dodd's people were on the job. I think maybe you ought to find time to have a little chat with Master Willis. You rank high on his list of people to be trusted; his father, you, God, and almost no one else."

"Be up as quickly as I can, Vicky. Sit tight."

"Somebody get to the boy?" Hardy asked.

"No way," Chambrun said.

"The young man's notion of what a soldier and a gentleman should do in a crisis," I said. "Betsy's in terrible danger, Chambrun's hotel is threatened with bombs. The only honorable thing for the Willises to do is face their own problems without involving friends."

"A fairly sound code of ethics, except in this case," Chambrun said. "Will you come up with me, Mark? I think you may rate just after God on the boy's list of the trustworthy. You got me for him when I was needed. You might persuade him to change his mind if his feet get itchy again."

If Chambrun could operate around the clock without any sleep, so could I, I thought.

"Give you a chance to do some thinking while we wait," Hardy said to The Man.

"To hell with thinking," Chambrun said. "What we need is just one solid fact to hook on to."

"I'd think of going public with this whole story, every detail of it," Hardy said. "You'd be astonished how often publicity and a reward offered will turn up someone who saw something."

"Offer whatever reward you think is likely to produce results," Chambrun said. "I'll stand back of it. What about our phony Mr. Gary? Could he be tempted, do you think?"

"I'm afraid you'd be outbid by the other side, Pierre. Incidentally, Frank Gary isn't a fake. He's exactly what he says he is, native-born Italian named Francisco Garibaldi, brought to this country as a child, name changed, father in the cab business, he changing it to a limousine service. He is married. The fake is Father Paul Callahan, and I'm convinced Gary played that role. But getting him to talk, even with promises of immunity, isn't likely. Once again, the other side can outbid us. But an honest person on the street who saw something, didn't think it was important till he hears the whole story—well, we can hope."

"What about the good old-fashioned third degree for Mr. Gary?" I asked.

"I'm afraid the third degree is pretty much a myth in modern police work," Hardy said. "Sometimes I wish to God it wasn't."

THINGS SEEMED quiet enough in Chambrun's penthouse, except that there was apparently no more gin rummy game in process. Victoria Haven was watching a coverage of the Beaumont story on television, outside shots of the hotel and crowds of people, an occasional interview with someone who'd been evacuated. Guy Willis sat by a far window, looking out at the city's rooftops, apparently not interested in the TV excitement. He looked up quickly as Chambrun and I came in, then turned away again. Guilty as charged, I thought.

Victoria turned down the sound on the TV set. "I'm sorry to bring you up here at a time like this, Pierre," she said. "It turns out I'm just an old woman giving advice to a man of the world. It just never occurred to me he'd try to go somewhere on his own. He's made friends with Toto, who let him go across the roof without barking once."

We walked over to the boy, who didn't turn his head again even when Chambrun put a hand on his shoulder.

"Want to tell us what your plan was, Guy?" Chambrun asked.

The boy hunched up his shoulder as if to free himself from Chambrun's touch. "I'm sorry," he said.

"I'm sorry you didn't trust me," Chambrun said.

I realized the reason the boy didn't look at us was that he was fighting that old problem of tears again.

"You scared the hell out of Mrs. Haven," I said.

"She's a very nice lady, and I—I'm sorry," the boy said.

"You're sorry, we're sorry, but would you mind telling me what you had in mind?" Chambrun asked.

Then he faced us, eyes glistening, lips unsteady. "Betsy's in danger and they're threatening to blow up your hotel, sir. All because of me. I couldn't let that happen to two people I care for. I knew the elevator wouldn't take me down without an okay from you, sir, but I thought the fire stairs—"

"There are men there to keep people from getting up, but also from getting down," Chambrun said.

"I found that out."

"What was your plan if you made it?"

"I—I thought I would get out onto the street, like all the other people who were being evacuated, lose myself in the crowd. Once I was out of the street I'd just wait for someone to pick me up."

"Someone?"

"The people who have my dad, and Rozzie—and Betsy. Once they had me, they might turn Betsy free and your hotel would be safe, sir."

"And your parents?"

"We Willises would have to face whatever they have in store for us," the boy said.

"You realize that these people who might pick you up want to use you to make your father talk?"

"That would be Dad's decision."

"And if he decided to talk, what do you think would happen to you then?"

"I know you think they wouldn't let us go because we'd know who they are," the boy said.

"Don't you think your father is bright enough to know that, too?"

"It would be his decision, sir. Not yours or Betsy's. You'd be safe and Dad would have solved the Willises' problems."

"Betsy will never be safe once they think she won't be any use to them," Chambrun said. "Your parents won't be safe once they've played their last card—you. Our one hope of keeping them and Betsy alive is to let them know that we're still holding you here, haven't made up our minds yet what to do about you."

"Captain Zachary said if you'd let me go he'd arrange to have me watched and followed, and rescue Dad and Rozzie and Betsy when they took me to them."

"But if you went out on your own, Captain Zachary wouldn't have been ready to cover you," Chambrun said.

"I was going to try to find him," the boy said.

"You decided his advice was better than mine?"

The boy pounded his fists on the arms of his chair. "I care for you and Betsy, sir! I couldn't let you pay for the trouble Dad's got himself into."

"Let me put it to you this way," Chambrun said, his voice very quiet. "I love Betsy Ruysdale better than anyone else in the world, boy. I admire your father and I owe him. But Betsy comes first. These people may still think they can persuade me, through her, to turn you over to them. For as long as they think that, Betsy has a chance. I appreciate what you tried to do for her and for me. But I can't let it be played any other way than my way. I'd have to live with myself afterwards, knowing that I'd cost Betsy her life by not following my own judgment. You understand that?"

"Yes, sir."

"Good. With that understood, let's see where we're at."

"It looks like we were at the foot of the hill with no path going up, sir," young Guy said.

"Smart kid," I heard myself say.

"How do you think your father would handle a situation like this?" Chambrun asked.

"Different than you, sir," Guy said. "You have people you can trust—Mark here, and Mr. Dodd, and Lieutenant Hardy, and goodness knows how many more. You can count on them. It's different in Dad's work."

"He doesn't have people he can count on?"

"Oh, I suppose the President, and Colonel Martin, and other big shots in the government. But what Dad calls 'the working stiffs' are different."

"In what way?"

"The temptations are too great," the boy said. "The people who want to buy something can offer so much a lot of people couldn't refuse."

"They could make the same kind of offers to people in my world," Chambrun said. He glanced at the old lady and me. "Do you think Mrs. Haven or Mark could refuse that kind of big offer?"

"Of course they could," Guy said.

"How do you know?"

"I just know," the boy said.

Chambrun reached out and touched his shoulder again. "That's how it is with me, Guy. I just know—know who I can trust. People who work for me feel they owe me loyalty, and that's great. But people in your father's world are working for their country, their nation, their government. Wouldn't you think you could count on them more than I can count on my people?''

"My dad says that working for a government is different than any other job in the world," Guy said. "A majority of the people elect a President, and they tell you it's patriotic to support his programs. But a lot of people didn't vote for him, and they'll tell you it's just as patriotic to oppose him. Salt that with a bribe big enough to buy a yacht, my dad says, and it can become even more patriotic to oppose the man in power."

"Your dad is a very wise if somewhat cynical man," Chambrun said.

"My dad is the greatest," the boy said. "I'm not quite sure what 'cynical' is, but if it's good, he's got it all."

"So now we have to concentrate on how to help him," Chambrun said. "Can you suggest anyone your father has trusted whom he shouldn't have trusted?"

"Gee, no, Mr. Chambrun. But I have to tell you again, my dad doesn't talk much in front of me about his job. Maybe he talks to Rozzie when they're alone, but not to me. What I don't know I can't tell. So I shouldn't be tempted."

"He thought you might sell him out?"

"No! He just thought I might be tempted to show what a big shot I am by knowing something important. But Dad would make jokes about some big-shot people—the way they talk, or their table manners, or their lack of a sense of humor. You have to deal with them, and you have to find different ways to communicate with different people. He'll imitate the way they walk, or eat, or smoke. My dad could have been a real good actor.''

"But you never heard him say he had his doubts about this one or that one."

"I've heard him say he was glad to be working for a man like Colonel Martin. I suppose that meant they didn't disagree on how to handle situations."

"Colonel Martin is on his way here from Washington,'' Chambrun told the boy. "He may have information about your father's job that Captain Zachary doesn't have. He may be willing to name names to help us. We've got to play it cool until he gets here, Guy. We've got to play it my way. Can I count on you not to take off on us again?''

The boy nodded, almost sheepishly. "Yes, sir. You can count on me."

"I'm going back down to my office, where any information the police, the bomb squad, come up with will come to me. Call me there if you need me for anything, either of you. If you think of anything, Guy, that hasn't come to you yet—''

"Yes, sir."

There was a sudden caterwaul out on the roof from the little dog Toto. Mrs. Haven went ahead of us to the door, calling to him. Coming toward us from Penthouse Three was Lieutenant Hardy.

"Toto!" Mrs. Haven shouted.

The little spaniel slunk toward us, muttering to himself.

"Thought I'd have another go at friend Gary," Hardy said.

"I can tell you didn't have any luck," Chambrun said.

"Bastard is just laughing at us and threatening lawsuits," Hardy said.

ANYTHING DEFINITE from the bomb squad was going to take a long time. They weren't just searching some key place, but hundreds and hundreds of rooms, private and public. The first places to be given a clean bill of health were the basement areas—the garage, the machinery like furnaces and air-conditioning units, the elevators. One place they knew for certain the criminals had operated was below street level, leaving Tim Sullivan's body and Major Willis's uniform stashed in the trash bin. Word was that we weren't going to be blown up from down below.

I had never seen Chambrun in the kind of state he was in as the morning wore on toward noon. The switchboard was being flooded with calls from, it seemed, all over the world. Everyone wanted to talk to Chambrun, and Mrs. Veach and her staff on the board were ordered to put no calls through except ones from Jerry Dodd, Hardy, Captain Zachary, and, believe it or not, Betsy Ruysdale or one of the Willises.

"You expect to hear from them?" I asked, not believing.

"They might put one of them on to me," Chambrun said, "to let me know they are still alive, and to threaten me that it won't stay that way long unless I do what they tell me to do."

"And you won't?"

"You don't throw in the only trump card you hold," Chambrun said. His anger was under such tight control it was almost painful to watch him hang on. "It's like the Black Days."

I had heard him talk about the Black Days before, a time more than forty years ago when, as a teenager, he'd fought in the French Resistance against the occupying Nazis in Paris.

"No way to make any kind of compromise or deal," he said. "Death at the end of every street and alley. Kill or be killed. But there are a million faces out there and no way to guess which one to aim at. Because I will kill, Mark, if it comes to that."

He walked over to his desk, took a small police special out of the drawer there. I'd seen that gun often, but I'd never seen it out of the drawer before. Now it was in the pocket of his gray tweed jacket.

Talk seemed essential to The Man as he walked restlessly around the office. "I never wanted any jokes or snide remarks about Betsy and me," he said. "I tried to keep our relationship as private as I possibly could."

"But it wasn't exactly a secret, Boss," I said. "There haven't been any jokes, and I doubt very much that there will be now."

"I've thought for years it would be bad luck for any woman to be linked to me," he said.

"For goodness' sake, why? There are hundreds of women who'd be delighted to be 'linked' with you."

"Like that boy upstairs, I live with a nightmare," Chambrun said. He fished a cigarette out of his pocket, and the hand that held his lighter wasn't steady. "Forty years ago I was a teenaged kid, already a member of the French Resistance, living in Paris, my native city. The Nazis were approaching Paris, and we were prepared to fight them in the streets, block by block. We weren't the army, but we fought and some of us died in a soldier's discipline. We killed the enemy, just as any other soldier kills the enemy. It was our patriotic duty, no qualms about it." He inhaled a deep breath of tobacco smoke and let it out slowly. "But I killed one Nazi colonel in a blind fury that had nothing to do with patriotism."

I waited for him to go on. He would tell me or he wouldn't.

"I was eighteen, but I thought of myself as a man, and I think I really was a man. The horrors of war and approaching defeat had skipped me past a whole period of growing up. I was a man—and facing death before I had to shave every day! And there was a woman." His voice was suddenly unsteady. "That woman was a sixteen-year-old girl. Her name was Michelle Furneau. I was passionately in love with Michelle, and we were adults in wartime. We lived together as lovers, but it was more like man and wife— total commitment. It was forever. And then the Nazis came!" He raised both clenched fists above his head. "Damn them, damn them, damn them! Michelle and I had to separate. I was a member of the resistance and I had to go under cover. Michelle had a job as a secretary in one of the big hotels—the Splendide. The Nazis took over that hotel, and everyone who worked there was suddenly their slave. A Nazi colonel named

Kreutz saw Michelle and decided she was to be his private property. What happened to her was reported to me by another French girl working at the Splendide. My Michelle was abused, raped, and finally shot dead when she tried to claw out Colonel Kreutz's eyes with her sharp fingernails. Nothing mattered to me after that but revenge—not the war, not France, not the Resistance. All I wanted was revenge. I planned it carefully. I watched Kreutz's routines—when he left the Splendide, where he lived, to go to the Nazi headquarters on Avenue Kleber; when he came back from work. I was waiting for him one twilight when he came back to the hotel from work."

I waited for The Man to go on. Old emotions were shaking him.

"I shot him, right between his filthy eyes," Chambrun said finally. "And when he fell I jumped up and down on his smirking face. He had been giving me, a French swine, a contemptuous smile, when I faced him and shot him. I was lucky. I escaped the bullets that were fired at me by Nazi guards outside the hotel. I had evened the score, but it was a hollow victory. There was no more Michelle."

What do you say to that kind of revelation? A forty-year-old wound was wide open again.

"Like that boy upstairs, nightmares took over my sleeping hours," Chambrun said. "It was a dream of my facing Kreutz, killing him, stomping him. It was a dream of Michelle being manhandled by that monster." He shook his head as if to rid himself of an image that was as fresh to him as when it had happened long ago. "The war ended, the victory was ours, the

Nazis were gone. But there was no Michelle, would never be anyone to take her place. Good things happened to me. I was working in the Splendide, which I thought of as Michelle's tomb. An American, Mr. George Battle, came to stay with us. He was a multi-millionaire who owned a great hotel here in New York—the Beaumont. He heard of things I had done as a member of the Resistance that had helped American troops at the end of the war. He took a shine to me. He offered to bring me to America, send me to Cornell University where there was a school in hotel management, and gave me a job at his hotel. I accepted. Anything to get away from the scene of my nightmares. There wasn't even a grave of Michelle's to care for. Her body had been dumped, like garbage, in a barge and buried at sea along with hundreds of other Nazi victims. The rest is history. I got to be manager of this hotel, and for a long time, every night, I dreamed of Michelle and Colonel Kreutz.''

"A horror story and a success story," I said.

"I've told you all this, Mark, so you'll understand a little better what's happening to me about Betsy. It could be Michelle and Colonel Kreutz all over again. If it is, then you'll understand why I do what I'll do. I'll kill the son of a bitch when I catch up with him.''

"I think quite a few of us will be ready to help you," I said.

"That's nice to know," Chambrun said. "But if the time comes, I'll want to do it myself—without help. I'll want this bastard to know, at the very end, who is paying him for what he did." He crushed out his cigarette in the ashtray on his desk and walked away to the window. "Betsy is a very special woman," he said, his back to me. "She cured me of a sickness that's been with me most of my adult life—since Michelle."

"Sickness?"

"I am a man, with normal hungers, normal lusts," Chambrun said. "But in the Black Days I had made a total commitment to Michelle. Permanence wasn't something I could offer anyone. I was in love with a dead woman. And then Betsy came on the scene to replace my first secretary on the job here. I never for a moment thought of her as anything but an efficient keypuncher. I had, long ago, made it a rule not to get involved with any woman who worked for me. That could involve the granting of favors to which some-one wasn't entitled."

"Don't mix pleasure with business," I said.

"And mark it down as a rule to live by, Mark. But Betsy turned out to be something special. She isn't just an efficient secretary, she turned out to be almost in-tuitive as to my needs and wants. I would ask her to do something for me and it was already done. I think I know everything there is to know about the operation of this hotel, about its personnel. Betsy knows it every bit as well as I do, and knows exactly what I would want done in any given situation. I admired her for this, grew very fond of her for this, realized I would feel lost without her. And then, one night—"

I waited for him to go on.

"One night, about three years ago, Betsy and I worked late down here in my office. We were prepar-ing a report for the board of directors for the next day. We came to some computerized information that needed to be assembled. I went up to my penthouse, and Betsy promised to bring up the figures when they were assembled. She brought them about forty-five minutes later. While I looked at them she walked out of the room, to the kitchen for coffee, I thought, or the bathroom. I finished the figures, and she still didn't come back. I went looking for her and—and there she was, between the sheets in my bed, naked as a jaybird!

"'Betsy, what on earth—!' I said, or something silly like that.

"'I'm sorry, Pierre,' she said. 'I thought I read the signal. If I was wrong, give me three minutes to get on my things and I'll be gone.'

"Well, of course there hadn't been any signal—but of course there had been. I had thought to myself, when she brought up the figures, how nice it would be, if it wasn't against the rules, to involve this lovely girl in something more than business matters. That was the signal, and she'd read it!"

"And so you've both lived happily ever after," I said.

Chambrun nodded slowly. "She asked for no commitments. She asked for nothing but the moment. She is a lover beyond compare. It has never intruded on our business relationship. There is no routine. It just happens when it's right for it to happen. Most important of all, my nightmares deserted me. Michelle couldn't possibly resent this marvelous, undemanding relationship with Betsy. Would you believe, Mark, Betsy has never guessed wrong about the moment?

She's never pressured me for attention when I wasn't ready to give it. She's every man's dream.''

"Most of us who might give it a thought know that you're her dream, Boss,'' I said. "We could grow old waiting for our turn to come.''

He turned sharply toward me. "You think if it was an even trade, that boy for Betsy, that I wouldn't make it? But they'd demand the boy first, and then they'd laugh at me when I asked for Betsy.''

"And you'd have given them the key to Star Wars secrets,'' I said.

"You know something, Mark? I really don't give a damn who has those secrets. What does it matter whether the whole world is wiped out from outer space or just from missiles launched from somebody's cornfield? It's total destruction for everyone on both sides, either way.''

"Then why not let the boy go if you don't care who has the secrets?'' I asked. "It could get Betsy back for you.''

"If I believed that was so, I'd have turned him loose hours ago,'' Chambrun said. He gave me an almost defiant look. "So now you know I'm not a great patriot, defending my country's interests. I just want Betsy back in one piece. If you think less of me for that, I'm sorry, but, God help me, that's the way it is.''

PART THREE

ONE

MUCH LATER I told myself that Chambrun's "letting down his hair," his telling me about the two women in his life and his real feelings about the crisis of the moment had been a help to him. I was flattered that he'd chosen me to be his confidant, although it could have been anyone else who might have been with him at the moment he had to turn it on. I think I knew it must have eased his personal anguish to tell me that Betsy came first and patriotism second. The fact of the matter was that if those values had been reversed— patriotism first and Betsy second—he would have followed exactly the same procedure. Turning the boy loose might force Major Willis to betray his country, but it would also condemn the Major and his wife, along with Betsy and the boy, to death. Whatever The Man said his priorities were, his actions would have been precisely the same. When it was over, whatever the outcome, he could never say that if he'd been a better patriot or a better lover, it might have turned out another way.

Shortly after that moment of what Chambrun thought was the truth about himself, Lieutenant Hardy joined us in the office.

"The farther we go the more likely it seems the hotel is clear of bombs," he said. "The critical areas, the basement and the roof, get a clean bill of health from men and dogs." He gave us a fleeting smile. "For a moment I thought a couple of those German shepherds were going to be annihilated by Mrs. Haven's Japanese gentleman friend, but she managed to control him. I just had a phone call from Kennedy Airport. Colonel Martin has arrived and is on his way here in a police car. Most important, Pierre, making the whole story public and offering a reward—ten thousand dollars, by the way—has produced results.''

"Somebody saw something, heard something?'' Chambrun asked. He sounded suddenly alive again.

"Something, nothing,'' Hardy said. "A man named Betts, Randolph Betts, who lives in the brownstone across the street from Betsy's building, came forward. His dog had gotten a short call in the night and he'd put on some clothes and taken the animal out for a walk. It was a little after four. He knows, because he quite naturally looked at his watch when his dog demanded an outing. He had walked the dog down the block, crossed over, and was coming back down Betsy's side of the street. He noticed a car parked there, motor running, man sitting at the wheel. Nothing particularly intriguing about it except that the running engine suggested the driver was waiting for someone. He didn't get a really good look at the driver because just then someone came out of Betsy's building. It was a man, carrying a woman—'slung over his shoulder like an old laundry bag,' Betts says. They almost came face to face. Betts asked what the trouble was, if he could do anything to help. The man laughed. 'A little too much party for the lady. I'm taking her home.' He tossed the lady into the car, got in with her, and the driver took off.''

"Face to face!'' Chambrun said. "A description?''

"A familiar one," Hardy said. "Hat brim pulled down over his forehead, dark glasses when it was still night. Could have been the same man described by your hotel clerk who registered him as Henry Graves, who claimed to be a friend of Major Willis's—without any luggage."

"Nothing more? Nothing else distinctive?"

"Nothing. Though I guess we can assume it was the same man."

"Mr. X," Chambrun said.

"Switch on your radio and TV," Hardy said. "I've given out the story of the girl who had 'too much party,' suggesting that it was Betsy. Someone may have seen her delivered somewhere."

"A very long shot," Chambrun said, his voice grim.

"I don't have to ask you if you have any better lead to follow," Hardy said. "If you did you wouldn't be sitting here playing this eternal guessing game."

"So we have Mr. X. or Mr. Graves, with his hat brim and his dark glasses, who claimed to be a friend of Major Willis's and got himself registered into an adjoining room. The same Mr. X is seen carrying Betsy away from her apartment building. You don't have to guess that he was involved in both abductions."

"And there is Mr. Francisco Garibaldi, Frank Gary to you, Father Paul Callahan to Mr. Cardoza, the Willis boy, and Mark a little earlier on. It brings me to the conclusion that Mr. X and Mr. Gary are just foot soldiers, carrying out orders from higher up."

"Why not let Gary make his phone call?" I suggested. "Maybe his lawyer will spring him and then he'll take us to the higher-up guy you want."

"None of these people are stupid," Chambrun said. "If we let Gary go he knows we'll be planning to have him followed. He'll take us somewhere, but it will probably be to the Bronx Zoo or the Aquarium."

"Pierre's right," Hardy said. "We're not playing hide-and-seek with kids. These people are playing for keeps, and they aren't amateurs."

"I've ordered Mrs. Veach to monitor any call she puts through to me that pretends to be from Betsy, about Betsy, or about the boy," Chambrun said. "I'll try to keep them talking while she traces the number."

"They'll guess you'll try that," Hardy said.

"You can't throw in the towel, Walter. You have to try!" Chambrun said.

The phone rang, and Chambrun switched on the squawk box. He looked almost eager as he picked up the receiver. It was Jerry Dodd. Colonel Martin had arrived from Kennedy and he and Captain Zachary wanted to come up.

"Stay with us, Walter," Chambrun said to the police lieutenant. "This Pentagon type is apt to put more stock in a police officer than an aging civilian with a foreign name."

"You underestimate yourself, friend," Hardy said. "But I'll stay. Officially, my murder case can be affected by what they decide to do. Whoever it is they're after on espionage charges, I'm after for the murder of Tim Sullivan."

I guess I react to soldiers the way millions of people have for years. If they're your soldiers, they're good guys. Out of uniform the soldier looks like any other civilian. He can be anything from your friendly doctor to a confidence man or a gun-toting gangster. His business suit or sports clothes don't label him the way a uniform does. I'd gotten used to accepting Captain Clinton Zachary as a tough, humorless military man despite his civilian clothes. Colonel Steve Martin was a little harder to pigeonhole right off the bat. He was about six feet tall, slim, suntanned with crew-cut gray hair, friendly blue eyes, and a smile that said "Welcome." Zachary made you brace yourself; Martin suggested it was safe to relax.

He shook hands with Chambrun and Hardy, nodded to me when I was introduced. I guess I was just "office help."

"We seem to have unloaded a miserable mess on you, Mr. Chambrun," Martin said.

"I didn't know you'd chosen my hotel as a battleground," Chambrun said. "I'd supposed it was the bad guys."

"Trouble has a way of following us in our business," Martin said. "We might have chosen your hotel as a base for Major Willis, but, as a matter of fact, we didn't. Willis wasn't actually on duty. He had a week's leave, chose to bring his wife and young son to New York on a vacation—shopping for Mrs. W., some big-league baseball for the boy, a little good jazz music for Ham himself. He played a pretty damn good jazz piano himself when we were in school together. Maybe your Duke Hines attracted him to the Beaumont."

"Have you forgotten that Willis and I had a pretty rough experience together about three years ago?" Chambrun asked. "We became friends. I owed him.

If he'd gone to any other hotel, my feelings would have been hurt.''

"Unfortunately your hotel, with its hundreds of foreign guests involved at the United Nations, is a perfect cover for strangers," Martin said.

"I don't think Willis and his wife were tricked and abducted by strangers," Chambrun said. "Someone he had no reason to mistrust trapped him, murdered my elevator man, stripped him of his uniform, and took him away."

"Romanov," Zachary said.

"Your needle is stuck, Captain," Chambrun said. "Romanov had an alibi."

"Which could be as phony as a Confederate two-dollar bill," Zachary said.

"I understand from Zachary that you trust Romanov, Mr. Chambrun," Martin said. "He's been on our list of people to watch closely for quite a number of years."

"Because he's Russian?"

"Partly. Your reason for trusting him?"

"Gut feeling," Chambrun said. "He's lived here for a couple of years. I have no reason not to trust him."

"You're not in our business, Mr. Chambrun, so you don't have any reason to think of him in the same way that we do."

"He's a human being, and human beings are my business," Chambrun said. "You're right, I don't think in terms of spies, but I'm dead sure that, whatever his game, Romy would not manhandle my Miss Ruysdale. It's just not in character."

"He would do whatever he was ordered to do," Zachary said. "Friendship for you wouldn't count for beans if he was ordered to go against it."

"So we come down to the nitty-gritty, Mr. Chambrun," Martin said. "Zachary tells me he has asked you to release the Willis boy, we cover him, and when the enemy take him we follow them to where they have the Willises and your Miss Ruysdale."

Chambrun had the impatient look of a man who'd been asked the same question once too often. "I have explained to Captain Zachary that, one: you can't guarantee they wouldn't give you the slip if they got the boy. They are professionals, just as clever as you are. Two: they know you'll be trying to tail them, and if they can't get clear, they won't take you anywhere that matters. Three: there is no reason to suppose that the Willises and Miss Ruysdale are being held in the same place. Miss Ruysdale isn't important to getting Major Willis to betray your secrets. She's important in forcing me to let them have the boy who could be used as a weapon. Four: if they get the boy to his father, whether the father talks or not, the ballgame is over. The Willises, Miss Ruysdale, and the boy will be eliminated. Our one chance to keep them alive until we can find another trail that leads to them is to keep the boy away from them."

"They could find another way to get the boy," Martin said.

"Not where he is. Not while I'm alive and in one piece, and while I have a staff that is loyal to me."

"Not if you are served with a court order?" Martin asked. He smiled a relaxed smile and tapped at his jacket. "Because I have one here, to be served on you at my discretion."

"I would resist it with my last ounce of strength," Chambrun said, "because I believe four lives may depend on my resisting it."

Martin looked at Zachary, eyebrows raised in an unspoken question. Do I serve it or not?

"For my money, serve it!" Zachary said.

Martin hesitated. "Let me ask you a question, Mr. Chambrun," he said. "The Willises left their suite, 17C, at about nine o'clock, leaving the boy watching the TV and with a promise to be back in an hour. We assume they were captured on the way to the Blue Lagoon, since they never got there. The boy fell asleep, didn't wake till one o'clock. That's four hours after he was left alone. If these people wanted the boy, all they had to do was go back up to 17C sometime in that four-hour stretch, ring the doorbell, and take him when he opened up to them. Why have they waited until getting him is so much more complicated?"

Chambrun frowned in silence for a moment. "'The best laid plans of mice and men—'" he said. "The Willises leave their suite at nine. Out in the hall or by the bank of elevators they meet someone they know."

"Romanov, probably with the Smythe girl," Zachary said.

"Or someone else," Chambrun said stubbornly. "They all get on the elevator together and then the 'friend' shows his true colors. The Willises are held up at gunpoint. My man, Tim Sullivan, tried to interfere and is shot dead for his pains. Now our killer has a problem. He not only has two prisoners he must get to a prearranged place, but he has a dead body he must dispose of. He can't just leave Sullivan in the elevator. All hell could break loose in five or ten minutes when it's reported the car isn't running. So they go to the basement, Major Willis is stripped of his uniform, Sullivan's body and that uniform are dumped in the trash bin, and they are off to wherever the prisoners are to be held."

"That still doesn't explain why they didn't go back for the boy in a while," Martin said.

"We don't know how long all this took," Chambrun said. "An hour? If so, then the boy could already have reported his parents missing. They had no way of knowing whether he had or not. In any case, they had Mrs. Willis and may have hoped her husband would talk to save her."

"We know she, probably both of them, were taken back to 17E," Zachary said. "That's where the brooch with the remnants of poison in it was found."

"Maybe the brooch was left there just to make us think Mrs. Willis had been there," Chambrun said. "Whatever they tried with Mrs. Willis evidently didn't make the Major talk. Now they have to have the boy. Our friend Frank Gary, playing the role of Father Callahan, is dispatched and comes within an eyelash of making it." Chambrun's mouth tightened. "A few hours later they play their next card, kidnapping Betsy Ruysdale and telling me what I must do to set her free—or else."

"And you'd rather face the 'or else' than let them have the boy?" Zachary said.

"I'd rather keep the boy safe than live the rest of my life knowing that I'd contributed to the deaths of four people while there was still a chance to save them."

Colonel Martin was obviously trying to make a decision when Jerry Dodd, looking grim, came into the office. He was carrying a small square cardboard box in his hand, along with what looked like a piece of wrapping paper.

"This came for you by special messenger, Boss," he said. "Atterbury, at the front desk, is just as bomb sensitive as the rest of us. Letter bombs are in the news every day. He turned this over to a bomb squad cop, who opened it. No bomb."

"What is it?"

"A cassette tape," Jerry said. "You better brace yourself and listen."

"To what?" Chambrun asked.

"Betsy," Jerry said. He walked over to the bookcase at the far wall and came back with a small radio-cassette player that was kept there. He took the tape out of the box and fitted it into the machine.

"You're not going to enjoy this, Boss," he said, "but I guess you have to hear it."

The tape began to turn, and for a minute there was no sound. And then Betsy's voice.

"Where is this place?"

There was no question about its being Betsy's voice. The man's voice that followed wasn't familiar. It was medium baritone, with a heavy accent, almost a musical comedy version of Russian, I thought. Someone faking?

"It doesn't matter where you are, doll," the voice said. "Your head hurt?"

"How would you expect it to feel after being knocked out? Are you going to tell me what this is all about?"

"It's quite simple," the comedy Russian said. "We want the Willis boy. If your Mr. Chambrun cares anything about you he'll let us have him."

"He knows?" Betsy asked.

"Of course he knows, but he's been very slow in responding. Maybe he doesn't care as much for you as we thought."

"I wish I was as sure of everything as I am of what Mr. Chambrun feels for me. But you're not going to let me go, are you, even if he does what you tell him to do?"

"You are a smart lady, Miss Ruysdale. I can't let you go, because you can identify me."

There was a scratching sound but no voices as the tape wound on.

"An erasure," Lieutenant Hardy said, speaking for the first time. "She mentioned his name!"

And then Betsy was back. "Don't count on Mr. Chambrun's playing it your way."

"So meanwhile we can have some fun and games, no?"

There was a quick, sharp "Stop that!" from Betsy. Then, "Take your filthy hands off me!"

"We might as well enjoy ourselves while we wait," the comedy Russian voice said.

Then a cry of pain from Betsy. "Stop it—damn you! No, I tell you! Oh God, please—*no!*"

There was a moment of silence as the tape wound on. Chambrun was leaning toward the cassette player, gripping the edges of his desk.

Then the Russian voice came back. "The rest is left to your imagination, Mr. Chambrun. I suggest that if you want to make it painless for your lady, you do as you are told. Turn the boy loose!''

"That's all there is," Jerry Dodd said after the tape had wound on for a moment. He switched off the machine.

"It sounds staged," Zachary said, "as though the girl was reading from a script, like a soap opera."

"No question that it is Miss Ruysdale's voice?" Colonel Martin asked The Man.

Chambrun, looking straight ahead at nobody, just shook his head. There was no doubt.

"It's Betsy," Hardy said.

"The girl could have been forced to put on an act," Colonel Martin said.

"How?" Jerry Dodd asked.

"Threats to Mr. Chambrun or the hotel," the Colonel said.

"Of course it was staged," Chambrun said, his voice harsh. "A man doesn't set out to rape a girl with a tape recorder running to record the act. Betsy certainly thought it was for real, but that creep with the phony Russian accent was giving an Academy Award performance."

Colonel Martin gestured toward the cassette player. "You don't think the attack on the girl was real?"

"Not what was recorded," Chambrun said. "After that—who knows?"

"You've checked with the messenger service that delivered the tape?" Colonel Martin asked Jerry Dodd.

"Of course. Kellog's Messenger Service," Jerry said. "It's got four or five offices all over town. Reliable—long time in business. The tape was handed in

at their office at Grand Central Station. They don't
have any particular reason to check on a customer.
They take his money, give him a receipt, deliver his
package. Wouldn't notice him unless he had a Rip Van
Winkle white beard on a W. C. Fields nose.''

"Or if she was a pretty blond girl like Pamela
Smythe,'' Zachary said.

"I'm awfully sick of your Romanov fixation, Captain,'' Chambrun said.

"Only lead we've got,'' Zachary said.

"So follow it up, but don't bother me with it,''
Chambrun said. He rose from his desk, as though all
his muscles were stiff, and faced Colonel Martin. "So
you have a court order to serve?''

Martin gave him a thin smile. "I think you've convinced me, Chambrun. Letting them have the boy
won't get back the people who matter. Question is,
what's our next move?''

"The only things we've got, Steve, are the boy and
that man Gary up in Penthouse Three,'' Zachary said.
"I don't agree about the boy. I think we should ready
a team of our best men, turn the kid loose, and hope
they take him to his father and our men follow him
there. You don't agree. So the only thing I can suggest is that we turn a team of our best interrogators on
Frank Gary, keep at him, round the clock, until he
cracks.''

"And if he's innocent and doesn't crack?'' Martin
asked.

"He was Father Paul Callahan,'' I said.

"I'll buy it,'' Colonel Martin said. "Your opinion,
Mr. Chambrun?''

"It's a way to keep busy," Chambrun said. "My opinion is that Mr. Francisco Garibaldi-Gary won't crack unless you use hot irons on him. But if that will keep Captain Zachary from concentrating on Romy Romanov and his lady, it would be a step forward."

"Remind me, when this case is over, to tell you what I think of you," Zachary said.

"No problem," Chambrun said. "I'll be wanting to tell you what I think of you."

"All right gentlemen, it's time to do something positive," Martin said.

THE TWO Intelligence officers took off to put together an interrogation team to deal with Frank Gary. Chambrun explained that the men selected would have to be identified to him and Jerry Dodd and the security men on the elevator and the fire stairs.

"You weren't very talkative, Walter," Chambrun said to Lieutenant Hardy, who was left with Jerry and me in the office.

"There's one thing I've learned in my business," Hardy said. "Don't argue with a man who's decided he has everything wrapped up. In your friend Zachary's case, he doesn't have a shred of evidence against Romanov, just a hunch."

Chambrun's smile was a bitter little twist. "Me too," he said.

"And you don't buy this working over of Gary routine?"

"It must drive Zachary crazy to have me say that I have a hunch it won't work. Tell me, Walter, are my priorities out of whack? I care first for Betsy's safety, then for Ham Willis's safety, then the boy, and finally Mrs. Willis. God help us, it may already be too late for her.''

''The convenient thing about your priorities, Pierre,'' the Lieutenant said, ''is that if you handle one of them correctly, they'll all come out right. It doesn't matter which one comes first in your emotions. It's different with Zachary and Martin.''

''In what way?''

''They have only one goal, only one thing that matters,'' Hardy said. ''They want to keep their Star Wars secrets out of enemy hands. At any cost, you understand. They don't care about rescuing Major Willis except to keep him from talking. If the Major should refuse to cave in and the bad guys kill him, Martin, Zachary, and company will have won the war and give the Major a posthumous medal for bravery and patriotism. If the Major talks, what happens to him and his family—and your Betsy—won't matter. They'll be asked some pretty embarrassing questions by the top brass as to how they screwed up. You see different things under your magnifying glass than they do under theirs. You see people, they see military secrets. Flesh and blood versus scientific formulas.''

Chambrun's frown deepened. ''To be fair to them, let's say they think they see the end of the world!''

''One man, Major Willis, can't keep that much vital information stored in his memory—unless he's a human computer,'' Hardy said. ''But there are other questions to be answered, Pierre.''

''Such as?''

''You can't just sit here and wait for your world to collapse, friend. What do you propose to do next, and what can I and the resources at my disposal do to help you?"

"You have a murder to solve," Chambrun said. "Solve it and you'll have provided me with all the help I need."

"It's not quite that simple," Hardy said. "We think we know what happened. We think the Willises got on that elevator at seventeen with someone they had no reason to doubt. That someone pulls a gun on them and Tim Sullivan tries to interfere and is killed. He can never tell us who the man was—if he knew. He can never describe him to us. The only people who can help us in this respect are the Willises. So we're both after the same thing. We happen to agree that letting the killers have the boy will get us nowhere. So, if not that, what, Pierre?"

"There is Frank Gary, who may crack under a tough interrogation, and there is the man who registered as Henry Graves, took possession of 17E where, later, Mrs. Willis's brooch was found, and who probably was the man who carried Betsy out of her apartment building. Note the word 'probably.' Men with snap-brim hats and dark glasses are not too uncommon. The minute we let people back into the hotel, this character can circulate right under our noses without our having the slightest clue as to how to pick him out."

"So it really narrows down to Frank Gary, who, your hunch tells you, won't break under questioning."

"Not questioning by Zachary," Chambrun said, "who wants to pin the whole thing on Romy Romanov. The real problem, Walter, is not to convince ourselves of who's involved, but how to force them to get us to Betsy and the Willises before it's too late.''

"We've done the only practical thing I can think of," Hardy said. "We've offered a reward. We can increase it. But the only way we can tempt someone to help us is to let them know we're tempting them.''

"Meaning?"

"Enlist every branch of the media we can reach to collaborate with us—newspapers, radio, television. How big a reward can we offer?''

"The sky's the limit," Chambrun said.

"How high is the sky?"

"Six figures," Chambrun said. "Half a million dollars if someone produces information that gets Betsy and the Willises back alive.''

"That will be your job, won't it, Mark?" Hardy asked, turning to me. "Can you set up a press conference in the Grand Ballroom, say an hour from now? Reporters will risk their necks for a story, even if the bomb squad hasn't given the hotel a clean bill of health by then. You, Pierre, and young Guy Willis make a plea for help.''

"You want me to bring the boy down from the roof?" Chambrun asked.

"I'll provide you with a regiment of cops to bring him down and get him back up there," Hardy said. "We offer a half-million-dollar reward, promise confidentiality to anyone who can point the way to Betsy and the Willises—but they can't wait till next Christmas!''

"And the information has to produce results," Chambrun said.

"Of course. No results, no reward," Hardy said.

Chambrun took a deep breath. "Done!" he said.

"Set it up just as fast as you can, Mark," Hardy said to me.

PERHAPS I SHOULD correct an impression I may have given. Chambrun wasn't putting up half a million dollars of his own money as a reward. I don't think he'd accumulated anything like that amount of money over the years. But he had many friends on whom he could count to come to bat for him.

One thing was certain. He wasn't going to pay a monstrous reward for gossip or hearsay. He would only pay for something worth paying for. My job was to get the top media people together for this proposed press conference. It wasn't the instant business that it would have been under other circumstances. Key people were not in the offices, and no one at those offices knew exactly where they could be located. They were all covering the Beaumont story, and like hundreds of other people, they had all been pushed out onto the street to wait for the bomb squad to sound the all clear.

Outside the hotel was a kind of quiet chaos. Hundreds had been evacuated from the hotel, to be joined outside by thousands of others who'd been listening to their radios or watching their televisions. They were packed together, staring up, waiting for the forty-story hotel to come tumbling down. A small army of cops guarded each of the three entrances to the hotel and, I suspected, the ramp on the side street that led down into the basement garage.

Lieutenant Hardy, anticipating all this, went out onto the street with me. I guess he knew that if he wasn't with me I wouldn't be able to get back into the hotel for my own press conference.

Reporters hadn't wanted to leave the hotel. That's where the action was. I got lucky. The police sergeant in charge of the Fifth Avenue entrance was able to locate Rex Chandler for me. Rex is one of the top television newsmen, rating along with Dan Rather and Walter Cronkite in the old days. I had had dealings with him many times in the past, setting up interviews for him with famous guests of the hotel, tipping him off to informal gatherings in one of the bars, restaurants, or private dining rooms, in return for information from him about foreign visitors to the United Nations who were staying with us, information important to Chambrun for his files on individual patrons. Rex had taken over a small beauty salon across the street from the Beaumont. I don't know if he knew the lady proprietor, or if she just found it exciting to be helping a famous newsman. Anyway Rex was in the shop, watching the hotel through its plate-glass window, holding the shop's telephone. He was apparently making a running comment which was undoubtedly being broadcast on his network. A cameraman was stationed a few feet away from him, taking pictures of Rex and probably of the crowd outside.

"We're in luck, ladies and gentleman," I heard him say into the phone. "Mark Haskell, public relations man for the Beaumont, and Lieutenant Hardy, homicide man in charge of the Sullivan murder, have just come into the shop." He gave me a big grin. "You're on the air, Mark." He held out the phone toward me.

"I need to talk to you in private, Rex," I said. I don't know if I've described Rex. He's tall, athletic-looking, with blond hair worn rather thick around his collar line, and with a warm and ingratiating smile. He knew how to take the stage, and he was on camera.

"We're setting up a press conference in the ballroom," I said, wondering if I looked as deadbeat as I felt. "Interviews with Chambrun, the Willis boy, Colonel Martin, head of Air Force Intelligence. The problem is to get you and all the other news people gathered there as quickly as possible."

"That's all we've been trying to do for the last couple of hours," Rex said, still for the public. "Get back in the hotel."

"The quicker the better," I said. "Cameras, sound equipment, the works. There'll be statements and interviews with Chambrun and the others. And we're posting a five-hundred-thousand-dollar reward for information leading to the safe return of Major Willis and his wife, and Betsy Ruysdale."

"Out of my way, man!" Rex said. "You want hurry, you'll get hurry." Then, into the phone, "I'm leaving the air now, ladies and gentlemen. I'll be back as soon as we're set up for this press conference Mark Haskell has promised us. Until then—thanks for being with us." He put the phone down. "How do we get back into the hotel?" he asked Hardy.

"A legitimate press card will get your people in," Hardy told him.

"Half a million bucks!" Rex Chandler said. "Who's putting up that kind of money? Don't tell me. Chambrun and his friends! Your boss knows the right people, Mark."

"You want a press conference, or do you want to chew the fat?" I asked him.

"On my way!" Rex said.

Suddenly people outside that beauty shop knew who I was. I suppose there were dozens of portable radios in the crowd with people all around them listening to Rex Chandler's running commentary. What kind of information would earn them a half million bucks? Did we have any reason to believe that the people who'd been kidnapped were still alive? And on and on...

All I could do was tell them to listen to the press conference that was coming up. Those questions would be answered, and many more. It took Hardy's help and a wedge of policemen to get me back inside the Beaumont. I found myself wondering if Betsy and the Willises were being allowed to watch all this on some television set in some secret place. Unfortunately for them they'd know whether what we were doing was futile and hopeless as far as they were concerned.

Inside the hotel the staff all seemed to be in place, obviously alerted. In some cases we were at double strength. Atterbury, the head day clerk, was at the front desk, and with him Karl Nevers, the night clerk. John Thacker, the day bell captain was at his post, with Mike Maggio, his night replacement, alongside. Mr. Cardoza was hovering outside the Blue Lagoon, not open at this time of day. The maitre d' was covering what he must have thought of as his nightclub. The staff was ready for whatever.

Hardy and I stopped to talk to the two bell captains.

"You two must know these press people pretty well," Hardy said.

"I plan to send my kid through college from the tips I get from them," Johnny Thacker said. "I'm to pass along any dirt I can pick up about famous guests."

Mike Maggio grinned. "You understand, we take the money, but we never happen to come up with any dirt."

"They're going to start swarming in here presently," Hardy said. "There may be some people who don't belong."

"There are bound to be gate-crashers," Mike said.

"You spot any, just point them out to me," Hardy said.

"You don't want us to give 'em the bum's rush?"

"I want to do that—after I've talked to them," Hardy said.

It was my job to report to Chambrun that we were about ready to roll. Johnny and Mike reported that the ballroom was set and waiting. I stopped in my apartment on the second floor on the way to Chambrun's office. When I took a look at myself in the mirror on the back of the bathroom door, I was shocked. I needed a shave and I was wearing the same suit, shirt, and tie I'd started the evening with—was it a year ago? It felt like it. In a few minutes I would be appearing on national television, looking like the local rag-picker if I didn't do something about it.

My electric shaver does a quick job of it. I got myself a clean shirt and a different tie, and a freshly pressed suit out of the closet. I found myself weighted down with doubts as I went through the options of making myself into a new man. We were running out of time like water running through a sieve. How long could the enemy hold Major Willis and his wife—and

Betsy—once a countrywide man-hunt was launched? They'd have plenty of time to make an escape move after they knew what the press conference had to offer. And they would know the minute the reward money was offered. Someone on their side might defect, someone may just possibly have seen something and the reward would revive their memory. Would they just sit and wait for us to stumble on something that would let us close in? Were we shortening the time that Betsy and the Willises had by staging a big public hoopla? Had we let ourselves be stampeded into a mistake?

Chambrun had once made a joke about me that could still raise a laugh in a crowd. He said, "Mark falls in love forever every six months." What he didn't know—or did he?—was that I had only fallen in love forever once, and to a woman I couldn't have. Her name was Betsy Ruysdale, and thinking about her was creating an intolerable knot of pain in my midsection. I wanted to be out there doing something heroic, and all I could do was try to make a press conference run smoothly. What must Chambrun, who loved her and was loved in return, be feeling? He'd said he would kill if Betsy was hurt, and I wanted to stand right beside him, swinging away on my own. When I got to Chambrun's office I found a girl from the stenographic pool presiding at Betsy's desk. She informed me that Chambrun wasn't in his private office.

"He's gone up to his penthouse to get the Willis boy ready for the press conference," she told me. "You think it will work, Mr. Haskell?"

"It better," I said. "We don't have much else to play with."

"Boy, I wish I knew something! A half a million bucks!"

I had the uncomfortable feeling that thousands of people were going to remember something that "just might be important." We were going to be flooded, I guessed, with useless or made-up nothings. Still, I told myself, there could be a needle somewhere in the haystack.

The ballroom was nearly ready to be filled with the ladies and gentlemen of the media when I got there. Cameras and special lights were being set up, focusing on what was normally the bandstand. That's where Chambrun and the others who were to speak or answer questions would be stationed. They would be the stars of this performance.

Rex Chandler seemed to be supervising the preparations, but a small army of nameless technicians were doing the actual work. Rex finally signaled to me, and I joined him.

"Ready when you are," he said. "We can't wait for the late stragglers coming in. So produce The Man, the Willis kid, and whoever else is going to answer questions."

Hardy, Colonel Martin and Captain Zachary, and Jerry Dodd were already on the bandstand when Chambrun made his entrance. He was surrounded by so many uniformed cops that Guy Willis, walking beside him, was almost invisible to the waiting reporters.

"Take away that gang of cops and somebody would have a clear shot at the kid," Rex Chandler said.

"One of your reporters?" I asked.

"Who knows—at today's prices," Rex said.

"They need the boy alive, not dead," I said. "What we have to guard against is an abduction. It won't happen here, with Hardy's men everywhere."

"What's old Mrs. Haven doing here?" Rex asked.

For the first time I noticed Victoria Haven's scarlet hairpiece—I think it is a hairpiece—in the center of the army of cops.

"She's been baby-sitting the kid," I told Rex. "Chambrun probably thought young Willis would need someone he could call a friend during this ordeal."

Chambrun stepped forward to centerstage and held up his hands for silence. The babble subsided to a whisper.

"I don't have to introduce myself to most of you," The Man said, "but in case there are a few out-of-town or foreign reporters present, I am Pierre Chambrun, manager of the Beaumont. Most of you are up to date on the situation here: the disappearance of Major Willis and his wife; the murder of an elevator operator, Tim Sullivan; the discovery of Sullivan's body and Major Willis's army uniform in a trash bin in the basement; the abduction of my secretary, Miss Ruysdale, intended to force me to let them have the Willis boy to use against his father; and finally, a bomb threat against the hotel, another threat intended to force me to turn this young boy over to his father's enemies. Since all that, there has been one more move, a cassette tape sent to me by special messenger. I'm going to play it for you now. The woman's voice, without any question, is Miss Ruysdale's."

He signaled to someone in the wings, and they could all hear the scratching sound as the tape began to turn—hear it over the loudspeakers set up in the ballroom. Then Betsy's voice:

"Where is this place?"

Then the comic Russian: "It doesn't matter where you are, doll."

And then it went on, about why she was being held, to force Chambrun to release the boy; Betsy's confidence that Chambrun wouldn't knuckle under. And then the voice with the accent: "You are a smart lady, Miss Ruysdale. I can't let you go, because you can identify me."

Then the sound of what Lieutenant Hardy had called "an erasure." Betsy had named her captor, but we would never hear it. Then the man again: "So meanwhile we can have some fun and games, no?"

Betsy: "Stop that! Take your filthy hands off me!"

"We might as well enjoy ourselves while we're at it."

"Stop it—damn you! No, I tell you! Oh God, please—no!"

The scratching tape and then the final warning from the man with the accent. "The rest is left to your imagination, Mr. Chambrun. I suggest that if you want to make it painless for your lady, you do as you are told. Turn the boy loose!"

Voices rose in a clamor of excitement. Questions were shouted at Chambrun. He held up his hands again for silence.

"Questions in a moment," he said. "As you can see, I have not knuckled under. I have not set the boy free. I want him to tell you why, so that you won't come up with a thousand time-wasting questions later." He turned to the boy. "Will you come forward, Guy, and tell them about the decision we made?"

The boy was sitting next to Victoria Haven, clinging to her hand as though it was a life preserver. She bent down and gave him a light kiss on the side of his head. He stood up and came unsteadily downstage to Chambrun.

Chambrun placed him behind the stage microphone. They'd obviously discussed this moment on their way to the conference, because young Guy didn't look to anyone for instruction. He took a deep breath and looked out toward the back of the room, as though he was speaking to someone special there. His voice was a little unsteady as he began.

"Dad—in case they let you listen to this on television wherever you are, I—I hope you're all right. They couldn't do you too much harm if they expect you to be able to tell them things, could they? Mr. Chambrun's right, isn't he? They want to use me to get you to talk. I—I was willing to take that chance, because I didn't think you'd want Betsy—Miss Ruysdale—or Mr. Chambrun to be hurt on our account. I was going to try to turn myself over to them, but Mr. Chambrun has arranged it so that I couldn't leave the roof where they are holding me, and so that no one can get to me and force me to leave.

"Then Mr. Chambrun made me see that the one chance I had to help you was *not* to play into their hands. I think he is right, Dad. However much I want to get to you and Rozzie, I now believe that the worst thing I could do would be to let myself be used to force you to do something you don't want to do—mustn't do. Please know how very, very much I love you, Dad. They're going to offer a very big reward for help in a few minutes. I'll be praying that it works, Dad. I promise."

The boy lowered his eyes and there was a little murmur of sympathy from the hard-boiled characters he was facing. Chambrun put his arm around the boy's shoulder.

"Guy will answer questions for you when the time comes," he said. "Guy mentioned a reward to you. We are offering a half million dollars for information that will result in the rescue of Major Willis, his wife, and Miss Ruysdale, and/or the identification of the criminals responsible for taking them as hostages. We don't want a million guesses tossed into the air, we want real hard facts that will lead us somewhere. Whatever you report to us will be held in the strictest confidence. There is a number you can call if you don't want to come forward in person. It is 1-500-HOSTAGE. I'll repeat that for you—1-500-HOSTAGE."

"Question!" someone shouted from the audience.

"Two more statements, and then you can have at us," Chambrun said. "I want to introduce Colonel Stephen Martin, Air Force Intelligence, and Major Willis's commanding officer."

Colonel Martin came forward, looking grim and forbidding.

"There are lives at stake here," he said. "I refer to Major Willis, his wife, and Miss Ruysdale. They are precious to many people in their own worlds. We are doing everything we possibly can to find them—in time, hopefully unharmed."

"You heard that tape, Colonel!" someone in the audience shouted.

"Yes, I heard that tape," Martin said. "It made me sick at my stomach. But I have to tell you there is something else at stake which may be more important to you and millions of people who will learn about this case in the media. Major Willis has information that could endanger the safety of your country if it fell into the wrong hands. Major Willis is a brave man. The efforts made to get at his young son make us believe he has held out so far. But he could have a breaking point. Most of us do. The safety of the Willises and Miss Ruysdale may not be important to you, but the security of the United States has to matter to all of you."

"Question!"

"One more statement for you," Chambrun said, shouting down the cries of "Question." "I want you to hear Lieutenant Walter Hardy, New York Police, Homicide Division. He is investigating Tim Sullivan's murder."

Hardy approached the mike from upstage. He was not a stranger in dealing with the press.

"Sullivan's murder may seem incidental to you after listening to Colonel Martin. But Sullivan had a wife and two children and what happened to him matters to them and to many friends who worked with him here in the Beaumont. But there's no use pretending that solving Sullivan's murder isn't a key part of this whole business. I want to tell you a few things we're looking for that could lead to your earning a lot of bucks if you have answers. So, here they are. The Willises left their suite on seventeen to go down to the Blue Lagoon. Somebody was on the elevator with them who shot Sullivan and took them prisoner. Did anyone see who went on the elevator with the Willises? Next, they must have been in the basement area later. So far, no one has turned up who saw them there. Next, a man registered here at the Beaumont about eight o'clock last night. He called himself Henry Graves, and claimed to be a friend of the Willises. He got the room next to theirs on seventeen. The clerk describes him only as a man with a hat brim pulled down over his forehead and wearing dark glasses. A little after four in the morning, a man who fits that same description was seen carrying Miss Ruysdale out of her apartment and taking her off in a car. Did anyone else see that man at any other time, in any other place? Finally, we have a man in custody who is Frank Gary, proprietor of a limousine service, who has been identified positively as having posed as a Catholic priest who tried to lure the Willis boy out of the hotel before Chambrun arrived to protect him. That's all we have, friends, but anything that would elaborate on any one of those leads would be invaluable."

"Question!"

Rex Chandler had apparently been elected or appointed by his fellow reporters to handle the questioning.

"I'll recognize you one at a time," he called out. "It would be a madhouse if you're all shouting questions at once." He smiled. "But I'm going to take advantage of my position by asking the first question. It's to you, Lieutenant Hardy, while you're still on deck.

How do we know the Willises were ever on Sullivan's elevator? How do we know that Sullivan's murder has anything to do with the rest of this case?"

It was a smart question, and it created a buzz of excitement.

Hardy smiled at the reporter. "I asked myself that question hours ago, Mr. Chandler. I got an answer from Jerry Dodd, head of the hotel security. Jerry, you want to tell him?"

Jerry appeared from the back of the hall. "Tim's body and the Major's uniform in the same trash bin made it look certain they'd been on the same elevator," he said. "But Hardy asked me to make certain. There are no elevators on self-service at nine o'clock at night. Major Willis wasn't a stranger to hotel help. The thing with Mr. Chambrun a couple of years back made him a kind of hero to most of us. He simply couldn't have traveled on an elevator without being recognized by the operator, especially in uniform. He didn't travel with anyone else, so he had to be on Sullivan's car."

"Thanks, Jerry. And one more unpopular question while I still have the floor, this one to Colonel Martin."

The Air Force man stepped forward.

"Is it possible that Major Willis arranged for his own disappearance?" Chandler asked. "That he sold out on you long ago? That while you're searching for his abductors, he's laughing all the way to the bank with a pocket full of Russian money?"

Before the Colonel could answer, young Guy Willis came charging downstage, shouting at Chandler. "Not my dad! Don't you dare say that about my dad!" He was clawing at Chandler, those dreaded tears streaking his cheeks again.

Chandler handled him gently, even before Chambrun got to him. "Listen to me, boy," he said, "I'm not accusing your father of anything. I'm just asking a question that must be asked and answered so we can get on with things. If we don't ask, suspicions may be lurking around us forever."

"I would stake my life on Major Willis's honesty and patriotism," Colonel Martin said.

Chambrun had reached the boy, and his protective arm was around him. "Why, if he is the villain, would Major Willis kill Tim Sullivan, Mr. Chandler?"

"Sullivan wouldn't do something Willis ordered him to do," Chandler said.

"Tim could only take him up or down," Chambrun said. "He could not take him sideways or to the moon! He wouldn't have objected to taking Willis to any floor level, penthouses or basement. Willis could have anything he asked for in this hotel. Let's not play games with this man's honor, Mr. Chandler. Let's get to another line of questions."

"So I've accomplished something by asking the questions," Chandler said. He turned to the audience. A hundred hands were raised. Chandler smiled and pointed to a woman reporter in the front row. "Maureen Lewis, International Network."

"To Colonel Martin," the lady said. "The classified information Major Willis is supposed to have—is it all just something that is stored in his head, or are there documents—written plans, technical designs, whatever? If there are such documents, you must have searched for them. Have you found them?"

Martin looked uncomfortable. "Major Willis has sat in on a whole series of planning sessions over the last six months. He must have taken notes. If he did, we haven't found them in his suite. He didn't leave anything in the hotel safe."

"May I add to your answer, Colonel?" Chambrun asked. "Whether there are notes or documents doesn't seem relevant to me, Ms. Lewis. The Major wasn't carrying documents like that on the way to listen to a jazz piano player. And the attempts to kidnap the boy to use him to force his father to talk makes it clear the Major wasn't carrying Star Wars secrets in his uniform pocket. If there are documents, the people who kidnapped the Major haven't got them, or they wouldn't be going to the lengths they are to force him to talk. You people are wasting valuable time trying to cast doubts on Major Willis."

Later on Chambrun and Hardy both agreed that asking those questions at the very start of the conference had been valuable. Intelligent reporters must all have had suspicions that Major Willis might have defected. Setting aside those suspicions at the very beginning had left them free to ask questions that might be important.

But as I listened to question after question directed to Chambrun, Hardy, Jerry Dodd, and Colonel Martin, nothing that I didn't already know came to light. Probably a million people who were listening to their radios and watching their TV sets were brought up to date on all the details we had, but no questions took us to anything new. I know now that while the conference was still being broadcast the HOSTAGE line was being bombarded with calls, most of them from crackpots, none of them providing us with anything new that mattered.

It was nearly three o'clock in the afternoon when it all came to an end. The reporters didn't hang around; all headed off to prepare their special stories and comments for later news broadcasts that would interrupt the regular features for the rest of the afternoon and evening.

I went back to Chambrun's office with him and Hardy and Jerry Dodd.

"Was it anything but a piece of show business?" I asked The Man.

"We can only hope," Chambrun said, "somewhere out there are people who really know something. If they heard, they know there is a way for them to get rich. They may have to think about it a bit before they make a move."

"So all we can do is wait," Jerry said.

"I find myself looking at people who are half dead from fatigue," Lieutenant Hardy said. "You, Pierre, and Mark and Jerry have been on the go right around the clock. You look beat." His smile was twisted. "I haven't looked at myself in the mirror. I'm suggesting that all of us go somewhere and get some rest—forty winks, or whatever time allows. If anything turns up except greedy people trying to sell us nothing, we can be alerted and instantly on the job. If something important does turn up, we'd better not be in a coma when it happens."

It didn't seem possible that we could just shut our eyes and forget, but I knew how badly I needed it. Except for some brief shut-eye when I'd been with young Guy Willis in Chambrun's penthouse, I'd been on the go since seven o'clock in the morning—of the day before! As far as I knew Chambrun hadn't had even that much relief. Jerry and the Lieutenant had been at it almost as long. Sense or not, I was eager to take advantage of it. Chambrun agreed to stay in the little rest room off his office. I went to my apartment just down the hall. Jerry and the Lieutenant went to a special room at the far end of the hall that was kept in reserve for the security staff. The proper people on that staff, Hardy's crew, and the switchboard operators were told where they could reach any or all of us at a moment's notice. I know when I got to my quarters all I did was take off my jacket, hang it over a chair, and plop down on the bed. I knew I couldn't sleep... and then I was gone.

It was still daylight when I opened my eyes. It was six o'clock, and I'd slept like a log for three hours. No one had called me. The phone is right beside my bed. I got up and switched on my TV set. The six o'clock news was on and my timing was perfect. They were showing a clip of the press conference. It showed little Guy Willis shouting at Rex Chandler and clawing at him. Drama in spades! Then the announcer came on to tell us that, as of that moment, 6:10 P.M., there had been no significant response to the rich reward offered for information.

I switched off the set, freshened up in the bathroom, put on my jacket, and headed down the hall to Chambrun's office. A different girl from the steno pool was at Betsy's desk. Seeing someone unfamiliar in that spot revived all my anxieties for Betsy.

"He hasn't stirred," the girl said, gesturing toward The Man's office.

I wasn't going to disturb The Man if he could still stay resting. At the other end of the hall is the switchboard, handled by four operators with Ora Veach in charge. The motherly Mrs. Veach has held her job longer than I've had mine.

"Half the world has been trying to get us on the phone," she said. "Most of them we had to refer to the HOSTAGE number. Mr. Chambrun got one from the people who have Miss Ruysdale."

That woke me up, but good. "When? What happened?"

"About an hour ago," Ora Veach said. "We'd turned away a thousand calls for him. Everyone who saw him on television wanted to tell him something. This one sounded different, and the operator who got the call put me on. Smooth-sounding guy who said he had information about Miss Ruysdale Chambrun would need to have. We had special orders for that kind of call, and I plugged in the Boss.

"'I'll keep him talking, Mrs. Veach,' he said. 'You get the phone company trying to trace where it's coming from.'

"We'd already set up a routine with the phone company, and I got things in motion. After three or four minutes I was able to listen in on Mr. Chambrun's call.

"'Let me hear your phony Russian accent,' the Boss was saying. 'Then I'll know I'm talking to someone who matters.'

"The man on the other end just laughed and hung up. There we were, listening to the dial tone. I told Mr. Chambrun I was afraid there hadn't been time to trace the call. He just said, 'Thanks for trying.'"

"You hear the man's voice?"

"No. Nellie Forebush took the original switch-board call, told me someone said he had information about Betsy. I got straight through to Mr. Chambrun. He told me to set the tracing in motion. I did. When I finally tuned in, Mr. Chambrun was telling the caller to use his 'phony Russian accent.' All I heard from the caller was his laughter when Chambrun said what he did. Then the dial tone."

"Mr. Chambrun report this to Lieutenant Hardy or Jerry?"

"Not on the phone," Mrs. Veach said. "But his office is just down the hall from them."

"He's supposed to let you know where you can reach him," I said.

"You want me to call him?"

I didn't. If he could have gone back to sleep after the call from Betsy's jailer, he was entitled to it.

As I walked out of the switchboard office, I ran head-on into Jerry and Lieutenant Hardy coming out of the security room where they'd holed up.

"After a while you begin to feel guilty doing nothing," Hardy said. "Anything at your end?"

I asked him if Chambrun had reported his telephone call to them. Hardy looked surprised.

"He must have thought it was just a crank call," he said. "Let's ask him."

"He still hasn't stirred," the girl in Betsy's office told us.

Chambrun wasn't in his office when we went in. Just to the rear of the office is the rest room or dressing room where Chambrun had gone to rest. There is a cot there, a change of clothes in the closet and a chest of drawers, and shaving and shower facilities in a little bathroom. And, of course, there was the ever-present telephone on a small table beside the cot. Chambrun was never out of reach of a telephone. The switchboard always knew where to find him.

Except at six-thirty on this particular afternoon. Chambrun wasn't in the dressing room. There were signs that he had been there. An ashtray on the table beside the telephone had a half a dozen crushed-out butts in it. He couldn't have done much sleeping if he'd done that much smoking.

Jerry picked up the telephone, asked for Mrs. Veach, and inquired where Chambrun had gone. Mrs. Veach hadn't been told anything, supposed The Man was still in the office or the rest room. The rest-room phone is just an extension of his office phone.

"How long ago was that call he got?" Jerry asked.

It had been about five o'clock, he was told.

The girl in the outer office had come on duty at four o'clock. She'd been ordered not to disturb Chambrun or let anyone else disturb him without special instructions from someone in authority. There'd been no such instructions, and Chambrun hadn't left the office, not past her.

But he had left the office. The answer was simple enough. There was a door in that little rest room opening out into the hall. It had a Yale lock on the inside, and the only way you could get in from the hall was with a key. In all the time I've worked for The Man, I could never remember him using that rest-room door. He is a man of routines, and I don't think he ever left the office that way because Betsy would be in the outer office and he'd always let her know where he could be found. Without Betsy there he might have chosen the most immediate way to leave, but he would surely have let Mrs. Veach know where he was going. But he hadn't.

We didn't begin to panic for about half an hour. No one had seen him anywhere. He hadn't been seen in the lobby area or in the basement, where police were still very much in evidence. He wasn't in his penthouse; nor, Vicky Haven reported, had he been seen since the press conference. He had chosen to rest in his office rather than in the comfort of his own quarters because he could get into action quicker from the second floor. He could be in any one of hundreds of rooms above the second floor.

"He could have taken an elevator somewhere, ordered the operator not to report seeing him," Hardy said.

"And that operator wouldn't report it, not even if God asked him," Jerry said.

But why?

TWO

By SEVEN O'CLOCK that night everyone who worked in the Beaumont had changed his or her focus on the crisis. Never mind about a missing Air Force officer and his wife, never mind about bombs, never mind even about Betsy Ruysdale, one of us. Where was Chambrun? Why had he broken all his rules, ignored all his regular routines? It couldn't have happened that way, most of us felt. Somehow the enemy had got to him. The only way they could get Guy Willis released, which they apparently felt was the only way to get Major Willis to talk, was on a direct order from Chambrun. Kidnapping Betsy Ruysdale hadn't worked. Now they would put the heat on Chambrun himself. How did they get to him? They couldn't have stormed his office. They couldn't have dragged him, bodily, out of the hotel.

"So he walked into a trap," Hardy suggested. "That caller suggested a meeting somewhere to talk about Betsy. He fell for it."

"Not the Chambrun I know," Jerry Dodd said. "He'd never let himself be suckered that easily."

"Who gets to be in charge of the hotel in his absence?" Hardy asked.

"Under normal conditions," I told him, "each department head handles his own job. Betsy would have filled in for The Man. I'd handle the press, Jerry security, Atterbury and Nevers on the front desk. But it's never happened—until now.''

This was an extension of the dilemma that had faced us ever since one o'clock that morning, when Guy Willis reported his parents missing. There wasn't the most insignificant clue to set us into any kind of hopeful action. The Willises had vanished into thin air, and so had Chambrun. We knew a little more about what had happened to Betsy, but once she was driven off in that waiting car outside her apartment building, she had vanished, evaporated just as completely as the others. We had Jerry Dodd's highly efficient security force, the Manhattan police, and Colonel Martin's intelligence people, all just standing around, hemming and hawing, because there was no starting gate pointing in any direction.

"It doesn't seem likely to me that Chambrun would do this to us voluntarily," Hardy said.

"He wouldn't," Jerry said, "except under one set of circumstances. They offered him a deal for Betsy. Part of his end of the deal was not to tell anyone what's involved. A threat to Betsy that he believed was real would explain a pattern of action that seems totally out of character."

"With the bomb scare over, people all moving back into the hotel, everyone on the staff must be super nosy," Hardy said. "Bellhops, room-service waiters, valet corps, maids, everyone on the go, seeing Chambrun somewhere wouldn't have been a notable experience. He could, quite legitimately, be circulating anywhere and everywhere."

"But now that the alarm is out, somebody should have remembered," Jerry said.

"If Chambrun wanted to go somewhere unseen, he'd know how to make it," I said. "He knows every back corridor, every emergency exit, from top to bottom."

"As I suggested before, he could have persuaded someone he trusted to cover for him," Hardy said. He gave me a thin smile. "Jerry and I have been like man and wife for the last few hours. I know Jerry wasn't enlisted, and he knows I wasn't. What about you, Mark? Are you Pierre's ally in this? Just say 'yes' and we won't ask you for details, but we'd know, at least, that he isn't in the incinerator in the basement!"

"The sweat on the palms of my hands is real," I said. "The answer is 'no.' I haven't seen or heard from The Man since he went to rest about three o'clock."

Jerry wasn't listening. His attention was focused on a little black box on the table beside the cot. "What an idiot!" he said, reaching for the box. "The Boss keeps that on his desk, a tape recorder. He has it there to tape phone calls in case he wants a record. He brought it in here in case he got such a call."

He turned on the recorder and we could hear a whirring sound but no voices. Jerry turned it off and opened it.

"No tape in it—if there ever was one," he said.

"It's routine for it to be ready to record," I said.

"Well, it isn't now. Of course, Betsy wasn't here, so someone slipped up. Or—" Jerry's face darkened. "Or the Boss took the tape away with him."

"Why?" I asked.

"That could get to be the title of a popular song if we keep on this way," Hardy said. "'Why?'"

THERE WAS NO ONE to go to who might have a clue. I had a decision to make. With the press and half the curious world wanting to get the latest news from Chambrun, his disappearance couldn't be kept a secret very long. Too many people were looking for him for the situation not to leak. If Chambrun had vanished against his will, the people responsible wouldn't need to be told he was missing. If he'd engineered his own disappearance, he had to know it would be public knowledge in a very short time. He'd left no instructions for anyone. He would have trusted Jerry Dodd, and I hoped he would have trusted me. Perhaps not Lieutenant Hardy, because as a policeman Hardy might have certain obligations to his job.

I wanted to believe that Chambrun had arranged for his own disappearance. That would mean he was in charge of whatever was happening to him. The fact that he hadn't left any instructions for Jerry or me could mean that he expected us to do the right thing. The trouble was, I didn't have the foggiest notion what "the right thing" was. Sound the alarm, or keep the facts buried for as long as I could? I decided I would only be playing with a matter of a few minutes if I decided to keep the lid on the story, so sounding the alarm was the answer. Before informing the press, I decided that Colonel Martin and Captain Zachary should be given a private briefing. If there was any choice to be made, those intelligence experts would have the soundest advice to give me.

Mike Maggio had already taken over the night shift on the bell captain's desk, and I instructed him to find the two Air Force officers for me.

"It's time they were told what's happened," I said.

Mike sounded grim. "Unless they're hard of hearing, they already know," he said. "It's all over the place like a brushfire in the wind."

Ten minutes later the two officers came into Chambrun's office. Zachary gave me a sardonic smile.

"Finally decided to make it official?" he asked.

"We haven't been certain what the situation was," I said.

"And are you now?"

"We've had no instructions from Mr. Chambrun," I said. "We have to assume that he's either been abducted, like the others, or that he's taken off on his own and expects us to react as though we don't know what's happened to him."

"Which you don't?" Colonel Martin asked.

"Which we don't. Before I inform the press, I wanted your advice and any help you can give us."

"Talk to your good friend Romanov," Zachary said, "and his pushover girlfriend."

"I've supposed that you people know more about the undercover climate we're operating in than anyone else; that you can give us the soundest advice on how to function in this kind of situation."

Colonel Martin nodded slowly. "The taking of hostages as a terrorist tactic to gain some kind of political advantage is getting to be as commonplace as your breakfast coffee," he said. "As we hear about it almost every day, our man is abducted to force us to turn one of their men we're holding prisoner free. In this case the demand is to turn that boy loose so that he can be used to force his father to talk. On the surface it looks as though taking Miss Ruysdale hasn't worked, hasn't forced Chambrun to change his mind about the boy, so now they go after Chambrun himself."

"That stubbornness of Chambrun's is going to add up to quite a total in innocent victims," Zachary said.

"I can promise you one thing," I said, "they'll never force Mr. Chambrun to change his mind, no matter what they try on him. He believes holding on to the boy will save lives—for a while, at least. He can't be frightened into changing his mind. He grew up, forty years ago, in the world of Nazi terrorism in France. He learned how to face this kind of violence long ago. You and I might crack under it, but not The Man."

"You haven't had any demand from them, telling you that they have Chambrun?"

"The last communication that came from them was at about five o'clock. Chambrun was resting in the next room. The switchboard put through the call to him. Mrs. Veach, the chief operator, was trying to trace the call. When she finally listened in, Chambrun was telling the caller to 'use his phony Russian accent' so he'd know he was talking to someone real. The man on the other end just laughed and hung up."

"Didn't Chambrun record calls?" Zachary asked. "You'd think he would. Isn't that a recorder on his desk?"

"It is, and there's one on the table by the cot in the next room."

"So there's a record of the call?" Martin asked.

"I'm afraid not, Colonel. The tape from that recorder is missing. The one on this machine is blank."

"So someone stole the tape!" Zachary said.

"Or Chambrun took it away himself," I said.

"Why would he do that?" Martin asked.

"No idea," I said.

"God save us from amateurs!" Zachary said.

"If you're referring to my boss," I said, "he's about as professional as you can get."

"Three people stolen right out from under his nose, and fallen into a trap himself." Zachary laughed. "Some professional!"

"I asked you to come here to give us advice," I said, "not smart-aleck talk!"

"At least Chambrun isn't here to prevent us from turning the boy loose and following him to where he's taken," Zachary said.

"Chambrun left us with instructions about the boy" I said. "They'll be carried out until he tells us something else, or we have some reason to think he's dead"—I felt my voice go unsteady—"and we have a new boss."

"The Colonel still has that court order," Zachary said.

"But he has to serve it on Chambrun," I said.

Colonel Martin seemed to be irritated by the cross fire between Zachary and me. He turned away, frowning, and then faced me again.

"We have been almost as lost as you are, Mr. Haskell, up to now," he said. "We have a lot of information about a lot of people you've never heard of. We've been following every single lead we have received since the moment Mr. Chambrun phoned me in Washington to tell me that Major Willis was missing. What's been happening since, first Miss Ruysdale and now Chambrun, is all part of the same ball-game. Captain Zachary and I have almost a dozen men covering all the people we have on a permanent list of suspects. It's just as important to us as it is to you to rescue the hostages—for different reasons perhaps, but just as important. Know that we're doing everything we know to do, waiting and watching."

"Once we know the action isn't taking place here in the hotel we're blind men in a fog," I said. "What can we do outside the hotel? Chambrun and Betsy Ruysdale are our people, our family."

"Getting a lead to where they may be is just as important to us as it is to you," Martin said. "I think you're right in giving out a statement to reporters in all the media. The more sharp eyes that are trained to look for trouble, the better."

"And after that we just sit here and twiddle our thumbs?

"Captain Zachary may disagree with me," the Colonel said, "but I suggest to talk to Romanov. If he's what Zachary thinks he is, he'll send you just as far off target as he can. If he's what Chambrun and the rest of you think he is, he might come up with something useful. He won't talk to us because he knows we don't trust him. If he's to be trusted, he just might come up with something helpful for you."

"Don't bet your last buck on it," Zachary said.

IT MAY NOT be easy for anyone on the outside to understand what Chambrun's disappearance had done to the hundreds of people who work for him every day of their lives. All of us had problems during our daily routines, decisions we had to make. There weren't a handful of people on the staff who didn't feel secure, knowing that Chambrun was somewhere on the premises, in reach of a telephone, and ready to back us up in whatever we did. He was what made the wheels go around, and suddenly he wasn't there. We were a ship without a captain, without a navigator.

In the next hour, while I prepared a statement for the reporters, had a couple of hundred copies of it made, and got it to Rex Chandler to circulate, I got a kind of sounding on how most of the people on the staff felt. The big question was, had Chambrun been kidnapped or had he arranged for his own disappearance? I think most of the staff wanted to believe that Chambrun was in charge of his own destiny, that he was immortal, so they chose to assume that he'd arranged his own vanishing act. Why? No one even tried to guess at that one. Better not to know why than to guess that he was not in control.

On my way up to Romy Romanov's apartment I found myself assailed by a collection of doubts about myself. Did I really believe what I was telling myself—and what so many others were telling themselves—or were we all a crowd of Pollyannas? Did we choose to let ourselves be convinced that Chambrun was running his own show simply because the alternative was unthinkable?

Pamela Smythe answered my ring at Romanov's front door.

"Oh, hi, Mark! Come in." She turned and called out, "It's Mark Haskell, luv!"

Romy appeared in the doorway that led from the vestibule into his living room. "Any news of Chambrun?" he asked me.

"You know?"

Romy nodded. "Your friend, Lieutenant Hardy, has just been here talking to us." He gave me a tight little smile. "Which team are you on, Mark? Am I a nice guy, or am I a sinister enemy agent?"

"I came here because Chambrun thinks of you as a friend," I said. "If you are, you could be helpful. If you aren't, I'm wasting my time."

"Of course I would tell you that I am," Romy said, not thawing very much. "If I'm what Captain Zachary tells you I am, I'll be playing games. If I'm what Chambrun thinks I am, I'll be going all out to do whatever I can to be useful. How does the saying go? 'You pays your money and you takes your choice.'"

"Do we have to just stand here?" Pam Smythe asked. "I can bring us some coffee or drinks."

"I make my choice, which is that you are Chambrun's friend," I said. "I'll stay with coffee, if I may. A drink at this stage of the game might send me into orbit."

We moved into the living room and Pam disappeared into the kitchenette. I looked at Romy—tall, handsome, his smile warming just a little. One of the most overworked clichés in the book is every man's assumption that he is "a good judge of character." Like everything else in this case I was believing what I wanted to believe, since it was too painful to believe anything else. I looked at Romy and said sternly to myself, "Friend!" It just had to be that way.

"I think I understand what you must be feeling, Mark," Romy said.

"If you have a better word than confusion—" I said.

"Here you are, in a familiar place surrounded by familiar people, and suddenly everything is different, routines changed. You are confronted by problems you've never faced before. It must be like coming to in a strange country where they don't speak your language."

"A little bit," I said. "We've faced violence here in the hotel before. Chambrun has always said that it was like a small city within a city. The same things will happen here that will happen in any other metropolis. But not to us! You understand that, Romy? While it was a spy story involving the Willises, it wasn't too far out. Now it involves Chambrun and Betsy Ruysdale, and that's the foreign language you were talking about. Are they in as much danger as I'm afraid they are, Romy?"

Romy gave me a steady look. "You think they may be tortured and then killed?"

I nodded.

"I'm afraid I think your fears are justified," Romy said.

"The cold-blooded murder of the Willises, Betsy, and Mr. Chambrun?"

"The stakes are high, Mark. The President's Star Wars program, if it's successful, could end up destroying Russia and its millions of people. They think of it as war, and in war you don't think of killing an enemy as murder."

"At this point I don't give a damn about the morality of it," I said. "I just want my people back safe!"

"They want to protect themselves against what they see as total destruction," Romy said. "A few lives taken in the process couldn't matter less to them."

"You sympathize with that point of view?"

"I sympathize with the masses of people all around the world," Romy said. "People who want peace, to be able to go about their business unafraid. I don't think I sympathize with the politicians on either side who see military victory over the other side as the only way of arriving at peace."

"In a highly complex, scientific technology like the Star Wars program, how can one man have so much knowledge stored in his head that getting him to talk could be so vital?"

Romy shrugged. "Colonel Martin and Captain Zachary may be able to answer that question for you," he said. "Like where is the fuse box located that can turn on or off all the lights in your house? You don't have to know how the system works, just how to start it or turn it off. One small bit of information like that could be stored in one man's head and be enormously important to his enemies."

Pamela brought coffee in three mugs on a silver tray. She and Romy sat on the couch together, I in an armchair facing them. The coffee was a godsend.

"If Chambrun has arranged for his own disappearance, what could he be aiming at, and where did he find a lead that he wouldn't pass on to the rest of us—and Hardy and Colonel Martin?"

Romy took a sip of his coffee, reached in his pocket for a cigarette, and lit it before he answered me. "I grew up in a world of intrigue, Mark," he said. "Understand, not that we don't live in a world of intrigue here in the United States, here in New York, right next door to the United Nations. But people don't talk and act as though they were living in a world of secrets. Chambrun may be a little different than the average man."

"Agreed, but in what way are you talking about?"

"I've heard him talk about 'the Black Days,'" Romy said. "Those were the days when his entire country France, was overrun by terrorists—the Nazis. Who could you trust? Who might be collaborating with the enemy. The end result was that you really trusted no one."

"What's that got to do with the Hotel Beaumont in 1986?"

"Let's say Chambrun stumbles on something that may point to the villain of this piece," Romy said. "He's surrounded by hundreds of loyal people, by the press, and by hundreds of others, foreigners and Americans, who could be part of a conspiracy to destroy the Star Wars plans."

"Americans?"

"My dear Mark, you're living in a dreamworld if you think there are no Americans who might sell out their country. A Russian spy in West Germany defects to the British and tells all; a British spy goes over the Wall into East Germany and tells all he knows. Why? Maybe just for money, maybe they have genuinely come to disapprove of their own country's policies. Americans sell out. Those people in the Navy last year—a couple of brothers? Whatever their reasons, misguided assessments of the truth or just plain greed, they are all around us."

"You're saying Chambrun doesn't trust his own people, his own friends?"

"I'm saying he grew up in a violent time when he couldn't afford to trust anyone," Romy said.

"If he told me something in confidence, I'd cut out my tongue before I'd betray him," I said.

Romy clapped his hands together in a mock gesture of applause. "I'm sure you mean that," he said. "But let me suggest a hypothetical case to you. Suppose Chambrun told you that he had reason to believe that I was the villain you're all after. He had reason to believe it, but was still looking for proof that would stick. You must keep this a secret until he had more on me. You wouldn't tell anyone, granted, but how would you act toward me? Would it be as it's always been, friendly, courteous to a hotel guest, relaxed and at ease? Or would you inadvertently let me know that I was suspected by a look in your eyes, the twitch of a nerve in your cheek, a difference in your whole attitude toward me? You could even be overcordial to hide what you now suspected about me. If I was guilty, I'd be watching for the slightest clue that I was suspected. If you, Chambrun's closest associate, were changed, I would instantly suspect that Chambrun, who could be dangerous to me, was onto something."

It made some sense, I thought. "But Chambrun would know what his disappearance is doing to so many of us who are concerned for him," I said. "It isn't like him to leave us all stewing over him. He could give us some other explanation for what he's doing that wouldn't show his hand—to you, if you were it.

If you're the villain and you haven't got him, then his disappearance must have you very much on guard.''

"Chambrun would know that," Romy said. "He'd be waiting for me to make a wrong move, dictated by my suspicion that he was onto me. That may be exactly why he's pulled a vanishing act—to scare me into making a false move.''

"But that isn't what you really believe, is it, Romy?" Pamela Smythe asked. They apparently had no secrets from each other.

"No, it isn't," Romy said.

"For God's sake, what do you believe?" I asked.

"I don't really believe anything," Romy said. "I'm just guessing.''

"Guessing what?"

"Has it occurred to you, Mark, that Ham Willis—Major Willis—may not be the all-American boy you all think he is? That he is the defector? That he has sold out?''

"No, it hasn't," I said. I guess I sounded impatient. "All this stuff about turning the boy loose so he can be used to make Willis talk makes that just about impossible to believe.''

"Does it? Try thinking the way the people in my world might think. Willis has passed on key secrets to the enemy. Sooner or later Intelligence will know that the enemy has those secrets and that they could only have been passed on by Willis. He wants us to think he was forced to talk. He may also want the boy with him when he goes into hiding somewhere. He's got plenty of people to help him, the fake Father Callahan, the fake Henry Graves, the man with the hat and the dark glasses, and heaven knows how much more.''

"Colonel Martin and Zachary have never suggested such a possibility," I said.

"Would they want to suggest that one of their own people is a traitor? They'd keep that very much to themselves until they can find Willis and nail him. The name in the trade for traitor in the ranks is a 'mole.' It would be a black mark against Martin and his staff if anyone guessed one of their people was a mole. They'd keep it to themselves until they could prove it and hang him."

"But you are just guessing? You don't have any real reason to believe that?"

"Who is doing anything else but guessing?" Romy said.

"Except maybe Mr. Chambrun," Pamela said.

"And he can't prove it yet, so he's gone undercover, waiting for someone to make a mistake," Romy said.

"Willis or one of his people, or maybe the whole Willis theory is phony and it's somebody else?" I said.

"That's true," Romy said. "But don't abandon the Willis guess, Mark, just because Willis once saved your Mr. Chambrun's life."

"If it was Willis," I said, "why did he have to kill Tim Sullivan, our elevator man? Risk hiding his body?"

Romy shrugged. "Something went wrong. Until it's laid out for us, we won't know exactly how Willis wanted it to look."

IF MY CONFUSION could be any more complete than it had been, Romy had helped to make it so. The Willis theory was hard to swallow, and yet I couldn't ignore it. It could be that way, and yet—Chambrun would have had a "gut feeling" about it. He would have bought it or discarded it. I had to worry about it.

Without Chambrun to keep the entire situation in focus, I realized that no one was in charge of the situation on the roof. Victoria Haven, tough old bird that she was, might just about have had it as a baby-sitter for young Guy Willis.

Betsy Ruysdale, Jerry Dodd, and I were the only people who didn't need personal clearance from Chambrun when roof security was in effect. I had no difficulty getting from the thirty-ninth floor to the roof, wondering as I went who would give the clearances now. Jerry, I supposed. He was head of security.

As I headed toward Chambrun's penthouse I was greeted by Mrs. Haven's "Japanese gentleman friend." The little spaniel snarled, and then gave me an "Oh, it's only you" bark. The last vestiges of a late sunset were disappearing in the west. It was almost eight-thirty.

As I should have expected, young Guy Willis was glued to the television set, where endless reports on the crisis in my world were interrupting regular programming. Chambrun's disappearance was already a news item. Mrs. Haven, watching the last light of what had been a grim day at the west picture window, turned to greet me with an unspoken question.

"Nothing," I said. "No news of the Boss."

Her face showed concern, the lines and wrinkles etched a little deeper than usual. The rumor that she and Chambrun had been an older woman-young man item years ago seemed reinforced by her obvious anxiety. She nodded toward the television set at the far end of the room. I don't think Guy Willis had noticed my arrival—he was so intent on the news broadcast.

"Hope keeps us all going," Mrs. Haven said. "It's just about twenty-four hours ago that his parents left him and never came back. When he tries to blot it out with sleep he has that nightmare of his, over and over."

"His parents being beaten by 'Father Callahan' and a man he can't identify?"

Mrs. Haven nodded. "He tried to force himself to sleep at first," she said. "He hoped the nightmare would come again and the second man would turn, so that he could see his face. It didn't happen, and he's given up. Has no one come up with a sensible guess as to what's happened to Pierre?"

"Most of us are thinking what we want to think— that the Boss has arranged for his own disappearance."

"I guess you'd have to count me as a member of that club," Mrs. Haven said. "But it's hard for me to believe that Pierre wouldn't have confided in someone! If he didn't, it becomes harder and harder to stay optimistic."

The TV was turned up so high it wasn't necessary to talk quietly so the boy couldn't hear. "I've come from talking with Romanov," I said. "He thinks Major Willis may also have arranged for his own disappearance."

"And that he's been trying to get the boy free so they'd all be together?" Her painted mouth was a thin red line. "I've guessed at that one too, Mark. But why didn't Willis take the boy with him in the first place?

Why leave him behind and then have to go through all this to get him released? At nine o'clock last night they could have all walked out and no one would have paid the slightest attention."

"To make it look the way it looks," I said. "That he's under duress, abducted by someone else."

"And have to go through the business of murdering Tim Sullivan and kidnapping Betsy, just to make it look as though someone else is involved? That's too farfetched for me to buy, Mark."

That's how it was getting to be for me—too farfetched.

"Are Hardy's people getting anywhere with Mr. Gary over in Penthouse Three—our 'Father Callahan'?" she asked.

"I haven't heard anything," I told her.

"They've been keeping at him," Mrs. Haven said. "I've noticed a change of interrogators every couple of hours. They don't let up on him for a minute. Does it do to you what it does to me—to know there is a man over there who could give us all the answers? Isn't there some new fancy way, some new technology, that can pry the truth out of him?"

"I guess the bad guys can be just as tough as the good guys," I said. "Major Willis won't talk, and they try to get the boy so they can torture him in front of his father. No drug, no truth serum, no machine. The bad guy can be just as difficult to get to."

Mrs. Haven turned to the window. Lights were popping on all over the city. "You know, Mark, just before you came I was standing here making two wishes. First, that I was twenty-five years old again, and second, that I was a man."

"Twenty-five I understand, though if I was wishing I could hope I'd grow old as gracefully as you have," I said. "But why a man?"

"Because, damn it, I wouldn't just be sitting here, I'd be *doing* something!" She faced me. "We've got the police department, and Military Intelligence, and the CIA, and God knows who else all at work like a herd of elephants trying to catch a garter snake in the back garden! I wish I was twenty-five, and a man with a hero complex! I wouldn't be tied up in red tape, or procedures, or the law! I'd be out there doing something to rescue Pierre, and Betsy, and the Willises. I've been in this room now for hours, holding a little boy's hand, watching that electric clock on Pierre's desk ticking off the seconds. Every second that goes by brings us that much closer to complete failure! And I'm just sitting here doing nothing!"

"You're helping that boy hang on to his courage," I said. "That's not nothing."

"While Pierre and Betsy and the Willises are waiting for some jerk's patience to run out! That boy won't want to live if his parents are dead. I won't want to live if Pierre, my last real friend still alive, is dead. Now, if I was twenty-five, a man, and a hero, I'd turn that boy loose, and I'd see where they take him, and I'd rescue the hostages! I couldn't fail if I was twenty-five—and a man!"

"I haven't been twenty-five for about ten years," I said. "I'm not a hero. But I am a man. Tell me what I should be doing."

She gave me a kind of strangled laugh. "You should be out there looking for the man who won't turn and show his face in young Guy's nightmare."

"Be serious," I said.

"I am serious. He's right there. Take off that snap-brimmed hat and those dark glasses and make him look at you, and you've got him!"

"There's only one problem with that," I said. "He knows by now that we're looking for that hat and those glasses, so he isn't showing up around here wearing them."

"Of course not. He'll just be having a drink with you in the bar and you won't have the faintest idea that you just bought a murderer a bourbon on the rocks." She shook her head. "Then optimism overcomes me, and I tell myself that Pierre knows who he is, and is waiting for him to lead him to where Betsy and the Willises are being held."

"But if that's true, the man knows the Boss is on his trail, and we've really run out of time," I said.

"I think I'd like it if you'd take your cheerful thoughts somewhere else, Mark," the old lady said.

THREE

IT WAS ABOUT nine o'clock when I took my "cheerful thoughts" down off the roof. Just about twenty-four hours before, Major Willis and his Rozzie had been setting out to listen to a little jazz piano in the Blue Lagoon. Was it possible they hadn't really expected any kind of trouble? They leave their kid alone to watch Clint Eastwood on TV and take off like a couple of youngsters on a date. Duke Hines's rendition of "St. Louis Blues" was said to be fabulous! A few minutes later Tim Sullivan was dead, murdered in cold blood; Rozzie had been separated from her brooch that contained a way of escape for her if things got too tough, and God knows what she'd been subjected to to make the Major talk. Or was not a word of that the way it was? Was it all a charade acted out to make us think exactly the way we had been thinking? I remember wondering, just before I left Victoria Haven and the boy, if young Guy Willis could have been in on the game from the start and been acting out his own star performance. I had what Chambrun would have called a "gut feeling" about it. The boy was on the level. The Major and his wife were on the level. Unfortunately my gut feelings didn't have the track record that Chambrun's did. Chambrun's instincts about a situation were never wrong. I was lucky if mine were right half the time.

My last words to the boy before I left the roof were half kidding. "You come up with a face for that second man in your nightmare, Guy, sound all the alarms you can get to!"

He took it quite seriously, promising he would.

The last time I'd wandered across the Beaumont's busy lobby without any special destination I'd been flagged down by Mr. Cardoza outside the Blue Lagoon to tell me he had a young boy in trouble. Right after that my whole world began to turn itself upside down. It was still not anything I'd seen before. There were people everywhere, going in and out of the bars—the Trapeze and the Spartan—plus the grill, and Mr. Cardoza was stationed outside the Blue Lagoon. But these weren't the fun seekers of a normal evening. These were rubberneckers, staring curiously at a bloody accident. This wasn't the Beaumont, this was the scene of the crime.

Many of those sightseers knew who I was and stopped me with a flood of questions. I decided I'd better get out of there if I didn't want to be buried alive. But as I was crossing toward the stairway that would take me to the second floor, to my apartment and Chambrun's office, I saw something else that wasn't normal. Johnny Thacker, the dayshift bell captain, was handling that job. Mike Maggio, the night captain, wasn't there. It was probably reasonable, I told myself as I approached Johnny for an explanation. Both men had been going at it round the clock. They'd probably flipped a coin to decide who'd handle the early-evening rush. In passing, it might surprise you to know how many people, literally hundreds, were trying to get rooms in the hotel, not for its luxurious service or its famous guests, but because it was bloodstained.

Johnny's explanation wasn't what I'd anticipated.

"The Boss had to have left the hotel under his own steam, or been carted away by a killer," Johnny said, "like Betsy. With all the ballyhoo on TV, radio, and in the papers, there are people who might be a little scared about coming forward with something they saw. There are people who won't go to the cops about anything. Maybe they have something personal to hide, maybe they're just anti-cop."

"So what's that got to do with you taking over for Mike?"

"Mike grew up a smart street kid," Johnny said. He gave me a tight little smile. "Maybe just a little on the crooked side, until he tried to lift Chambrun's wallet one night on a street corner. The Boss didn't send him to jail, he reformed him and turned him into one of his trusted people."

"A familiar legend," I said. "So Mike took the night off?"

"Come on, Mark. Mike is trying to find the Boss. There is an army of street kids out there who still think Mike is some kind of a hero. Mike's got them mobilized. People might talk to those kids, who are obviously not cops; kids can listen to conversations that obviously aren't meant for them. To a lot of people, a black kid carrying a shoe-shine kit doesn't exist. They'll talk like he wasn't there. Mike's got his army all over the neighborhood. Someone had to see the Boss walk away from here, or be taken away. It took Hardy almost a day to find the guy who saw Betsy carried off. We don't have that much time to find Mr.

Chambrun. He's too hot a potato for anyone to hang on to for too long. Mike hopes his kids may sniff out something faster than the police."

"He's told Lieutenant Hardy?"

Johnny shrugged. "If he ran into him he probably has. He wasn't going to wait to ask permission."

Somehow Johnny's explanation made me feel good. People who cared were working, not just cops doing a job. I had an impulse to go out onto the street to have a look at "Mike Maggio's army" doing a job.

There were more cops stationed to keep people out of the hotel than were working on the case, I imagined. There was no space in any of the bars or restaurants for more customers. It would result in a mob scene if they just let people in at will.

"You live or work here?" a cop at the north-side exit asked me as I started out. "You better be able to prove it if you expect to get back in."

"It's my address," I said. "Driver's license do?"

It was crazy out there on the street, people elbow to elbow, crowding, jostling, pointing, shouting. Every once in a while I saw a young boy milling around. I had an unkind thought about Mike's army. There would probably be a hell of a lot more pockets picked than information gathered. I hoped I might see Mike somewhere. I was too exhausted to think clearly for myself. Mike might suggest something positive I could do instead of just being a question box for some excitement-hungry spectator.

I hadn't gone more than a couple of yards from the entrance when I felt a hand on my arm. I turned and looked at a dirty-faced bum who was grinning at me. Then I realized it was Mike Maggio.

"Out for an evening constitutional?" he asked me.

"You had me there for a minute," I said. "Johnny just explained what you're doing out here, and I came out to have a look."

"Trouble out here," Mike said, "is that most of this crowd are people who came here after the fact. This mob aren't the neighbors who might have seen something, these are clowns who've been watching their TV sets."

"I think it's great, what you're trying to do," I said. "But is there any real chance it will pay off?"

"You'll never find out if you don't try," Mike said. Something about the look on his face under that applied dirt told me that he was hurting. He loved Chambrun, just as I did. "I watched the cops fumbling around trying to collect fingerprints to match against a master set they haven't got. I watched those Air Force characters playing their hush-hush spy games, knowing all the important secrets except the one they want—where their Major is and who took him. I watched the hotel which is my life jerked around by bomb threats, people I care about murdered and abducted, and Jerry Dodd isn't any closer than the cops or the generals." He drew a deep breath and hunched his shoulders. "So—I figure I can't do any worse than the others by coming out here in the street and trying to smell it out!"

"A progress report?"

"So far, not a whiff," Mike said. Then he stiffened. "Oh brother, there's one of my kids getting himself in trouble." He gave me a tap on the chest with his knuckles. "See you around!"

He was instantly swallowed up in the crowd, and in the dim light from the street lamps I couldn't see a trace of him or the kid who was "getting himself in trouble."

I turned back toward the entrance, the glass canopy out over the sidewalk, brightly and skillfully lighted. Under ordinary circumstances that lighted area was a sign of welcome. Now it was a gateway to terrorism and murder. Pierre Chambrun, who knew it so well, who managed every detail to perfection, from a dinner for the President of the United States to the mending of a cigarette burn in a back hall carpet, was gone. It could never be the same again if we didn't find him. Nothing could have happened to him in the hotel, I thought. It was absurd, but I found myself dreaming that the building itself would somehow have risen up to protect him. Doors would have closed that couldn't be unlocked, walls and ceilings would have crowded in on Chambrun's enemies.

When you start having such foolish thoughts as that, you'd better get away somewhere and try to make sense, I told myself. Better to get away from all these gaping gooks who were waiting, hopefully, for some butchered hostage to be tossed out onto the street for their pleasure, and find a quiet place where something really useful might take shape.

I walked slowly, just trying to ease my way out of the crowd, for almost two blocks before it began to thin out. I'd never have made it in daylight. Someone would have recognized me as one of the Beaumont's staff and I'd have been buried under questions. Oh, there were people, and the movement was all toward the Beaumont. I guess that's why I noticed a man on the other side of the street, on the far sidewalk, headed, as I was, away from the excitement. There was something familiar about him, but I couldn't place it at that moment. A reporter leaving the scene to file a story? Someone who just didn't have an appetite for sensation or a taste for blood? I don't know why I kept speculating about him except that there was something about him, something about the way he moved, that was familiar. There was no way to recognize a face, hidden by a hat brim in the semidarkness.

Then the man turned and climbed the five or six front steps of a brownstone house. At the top of the steps he turned and looked back down the street toward the hotel. Reflected light from the great city was evidently a little brighter at the top of those front steps than it was on the sidewalk. No wonder he'd looked familiar. It was Captain Zachary.

I called out to him, waved to him as he turned my way, and started across the street to him. My intention was to tell him about my conversation with Romy Romanov and Pamela Smythe. Zachary stood very still as I approached him, hands jammed in the pockets of his tropical-worsted jacket. I was close to Chambrun, and Chambrun and Zachary didn't hit it off, so it didn't surprise me that the Air Force captain wasn't prepared to give me a "good old buddy, buddy" greeting. His face had the stony look I associated with it, his mouth set in a kind of thin sneer.

"Just trying to get away from questions for a few minutes," I told him. "Saw you across the way and thought I'd report to you about my conversation with Romy Romanov."

"He provide you with some more alibis for himself and his little blond tootsie?"

"Well, not exactly. But some interesting suggestions."

"Well, let's not stand here," Zachary said. "Somebody's bound to recognize one of us, and we'll be swamped with questions again."

To my surprise he produced a key and proceeded to unlock the front door of the brownstone. Intelligence had probably taken over the building as some kind of headquarters, I reasoned. It was pitch-black beyond the door, but Zachary obviously knew where a light switch was located. It revealed the typical old-fashioned interior; a stairway leading up, and narrow hallway going back to a rear apartment. The carpeting was old, worn, and dirty. It didn't look as if anyone who'd cared for the place had lived here recently.

As we stepped in, the door at the end of the hallway opened and a man appeared. He was a big, heavyset fellow, wearing a dark blue work shirt and slacks, what looked like a day's growth of red beard on his cheeks, chin, and neck. What stopped me in my tracks was seeing that he was cradling some sort of automatic rifle or machine gun in his arms. As I stood there staring at him, I heard the front door close behind me.

"What've you got here?" the man with the gun asked in a deep, rasping voice.

"This is Mark Haskell, the P.R. man for the hotel," Zachary said from behind me, "either the stupidest or the unluckiest man in the city of New York."

I spun around, and he was giving me that sour grin of his. "You can call my friend Smith, or Jones, or

Brown, or Red. I don't imagine you'll be carrying on any lengthy conversations with him."

I felt myself grabbed from behind and subjected to a frisk for a weapon, which of course was a waste of time. I was painfully clean.

"You bring in very many more like this, Zach," the man behind me said, "and we'll have to start stacking them up like firewood."

"I didn't exactly bring Mr. Haskell on purpose," Zachary said. "Either he followed me, or I just got unlucky."

"Let's get this light out," Smith-Jones-Brown said. "Somebody may get curious if they see it from the street. Down the hall to the back room, buster."

I felt the muzzle of that gun jammed into my kidneys, and I walked. Things were spinning around at a dizzy rate in my head. Zachary! Was he the mole, the betrayer from within that Romy had suggested? If he was, I was no more stupid than Chambrun, or Hardy, or Colonel Martin being caught off base by a slick move. I felt a cold chill run down my spine. Was I afraid for myself, or for Chambrun, who may have been caught off base just as simply as I'd been?

The back room was a dingy little place, furnished only with a blanket-covered cot, a small kitchen table, its white paint peeling off, and three plain kitchen chairs, never painted. A single unshaded light bulb in a ceiling fixture provided the light.

Zachary's friend put his weapon down on the table, reached in his shirt pocket for a cigarette, and lit it with a lighter which he produced from his pants pocket. Neither he nor Zachary seemed to be concerned with the possibility that I might make a grab for that gun on the table. They were right. I wasn't about to try heroics. I wasn't sure, at that moment, if my shaking knees would hold me up if I tried to move.

"It doesn't really matter whether you got onto me or it was just an accident that you saw me outside this place," Zachary said. "But I'm curious."

"It matters," the gunman said, "because if he figured us out we may have the whole United States Army down on us in a few minutes. You sure no one else was following you, Zach?"

"Positive," Zachary said. "I'm not likely to miss someone who's intentionally tailing me, Red."

"There can always be a first time," Red said.

Things began to fall into ugly place for me. Major Willis and his Rozzie, on the way to the Blue Lagoon, could have met Zachary in the hall outside their suite. They might have been surprised, but would have had no reason to be concerned. Zachary was part of the Major's team, probably saying he'd been on the way with some kind of message when they met in the hall. They go on the elevator together, Zachary shows his true hand, and Tim Sullivan tries to interfere and gets his. Zachary could have been the man with the hat and the dark glasses who'd called himself Henry Graves, a friend of the Major's who was assigned to 17E, the room next to the Willis suite. At nine o'clock last night no one in the Beaumont had ever heard of Captain Zachary. The desk clerk would have had no reason to associate him with "Henry Graves." And Betsy— she'd have let Zachary come up to her apartment at four in the morning. He was a "good guy." And Chambrun though I knew he didn't like Zachary, would not have been likely to be suspicious of him.

"Are they all here in this building?" I asked.

"We ask the questions, you give the answers," Zachary said. "Had you gotten wise to me, or was it an accident?"

The only card I held was to keep him guessing. "Romy suggested we should be looking for a mole in your organization," I said.

"So you followed me from the hotel?"

"Well, I spotted you anyway, didn't I?"

"Is this one any use to us?" Red asked Zachary. "We can't keep nursemaiding more and more people, Zach. If he's no use to you, let's get rid of him and be done with it."

Zachary stood staring at me, like a kid studying a puzzling problem on the blackboard. "Chambrun is very soft about his people," he said. "This one could be useful. Let's hang onto him for a bit. Give him the treatment, Red."

I was grabbed from behind, my arms twisted behind me. I struggled, but Red was giant strong. I felt cold steel against my wrists and realized that I'd been handcuffed. I was spun around like a doll, and a wide strip of adhesive tape was slapped over my mouth, even before I could shout.

"March toward the door!" Red ordered.

Zachary opened the door and stood there, frozen, staring at Chambrun, who was pointing a gun straight at his forehead—the little gun I'd seen him put in his jacket pocket hours ago. Chambrun wasn't alone. Behind him in the dark hallway was a small army— kids, headed by Mike Maggio!

I didn't have to see Red reaching for his automatic rifle. It was Mike who moved, launching a vicious karate kick at Red's jaw. Red staggered away against the wall and Mike had the gun.

"Do we let the law have them, Boss, or do we kill the sons of bitches right here and now?" Mike asked.

"We take them in," Chambrun said.

The army of kids swarmed around Zachary and Red. Chambrun approached me.

"I thought you were going to blow the whole ballgame, Mark, when I saw you walk into the house with him! This is going to hurt."

He reached out and gave the adhesive tape over my mouth one swift jerk. It was the loveliest pain I ever felt. And then his arms were around me in a fatherly hug. I couldn't return it, because my hands were still chained behind me. Then one of the kids was releasing me. I suppose he'd found the handcuff keys in Red's pocket.

Chambrun turned to Zachary, who'd been given the handcuff treatment by Mike's kids. "I'll give you just thirty seconds, Zachary, to take me to the others—or I'll shoot your miserable brains out. I'll leave it to you to decide whether I'm fooling. I start counting now—twenty-nine, twenty-eight, twenty-seven—"

"Down in the cellar," Zachary said.

So MUCH HAPPENED so quickly.

A couple of Mike's kids went racing off to the hotel to find Lieutenant Hardy and Colonel Martin and bring them back with reinforcements. Mike, holding Red's repeating rifle in his hands, grinned at his two prisoners.

"I've always wanted to play with one of these," Mike was saying. "Don't tempt me."

Some of the kids found the cellar stairs, found a
light switch, and went down ahead of Chambrun and
me. I don't know what I expected, but whatever it was
going to be, I dreaded it.

What we found were three people, handcuffed to
uprights that held up the ceiling, mouths taped, eyes
wide and frightened until they saw Chambrun. Betsy
and the Willises were alive.

Chambrun was with Betsy. "This is going to hurt,"
he said again, and ripped the tape off her mouth.

"Oh, Pierre—I was such a fool, such an idiot."

"Not now—maybe next year," he said. "Right now
it's all over." He held her very close for a moment, and
watching was almost like an invasion of privacy. Then
he went over and knelt beside Mrs. Willis. "Take care
of the Major, Mark," he said.

A bright-eyed little black boy was working on the
Major's handcuffs.

"That boy could pick the lock on the United States
Mint if it was called for," I heard Chambrun tell Rosalind Willis.

"Guy—my boy?" I heard her ask.

"Just fine," Chambrun said. "I'll get you to him
right away."

I wasn't good at that quick jerk, but I got the adhesive off the Major's mouth.

"Thanks, Mark," he said. His voice sounded as
though he'd forgotten how to use it. "I was beginning
to give up hope—" The grinning kid who'd been
kneeling behind the Major came around, holding up
the handcuffs. The Major held out his hands, flexing
his fingers. Then he walked over to his wife, took her
in his arms, and held her.

There was a thunder of footsteps on the cellar stairs, and Hardy, Colonel Martin, and three or four cops came down.

"You got those two characters upstairs, Walter?" Chambrun asked the detective.

"Got them, but have you got something on them?" Hardy asked. "They're already screaming 'false arrest.'"

Chambrun just gestured toward Betsy and the Willises. Hardy wasn't going to have to worry about a false arrest.

A POLICE CAR carrying Betsy, the Willises, and me went around to the back of the Beaumont and into the basement garage. We took an elevator from there to the roof, avoiding all the reporters and sightseers in the lobby. In Chambrun's penthouse there was a touching reunion between the Willises and their boy. Mrs. Haven whisked Betsy off into the bedroom section to freshen up and indulge in woman talk.

My first impulse was to call the desk downstairs and release the front-line story—the hostages were freed and safe, their abductors under arrest. Then I decided I'd wait for a green light from Chambrun and Hardy. I decided I could use that drink I'd refused earlier at Romy's, and I went over to the sideboard and poured myself a slug of Jack Daniel's.

I should have guessed what Mike Maggio told me later. Chambrun was making a "God's in his heaven, all's right with the world" tour of the lobby. His people would know that he was back on his throne and in business.

The bits and pieces were put together about an hour later when the three hostages, young Guy Willis, Mrs. Haven, and Chambrun, along with Hardy, Colonel Martin, and a policeman at a stenotype machine were gathered together. They took it in sequence, the Willis story coming first. It was much as we'd imagined it.

"Rozzie and I had just left our suite to go down to the Blue Lagoon," Willis told us, "when we ran into Clint Zachary out in the hall. I was surprised, yet not surprised in a way. He told me he was on his way to find me, had some official business. I told him Rozzie and I were headed down to hear Duke Hines's nine-o'clock show. Could he wait for business talk till after that? He was cheerful enough about it, said he'd go with us."

"You knew who he was, Mrs. Willis?" Hardy asked.

"Oh yes," Rozzie Willis said. She was sitting on the couch, holding young Guy's hand in hers, beaming, a far cry from the haggard woman I'd seen in the basement of that brownstone a little while ago. "Ham and I had run across him several times in Washington. He'd even been to our apartment there—on official business. He was 'one of us,' you know?"

"In any case, we started down in the elevator, the three of us with your man Sullivan," the Major said. "Zachary told Sullivan to keep going down to the garage area. There was something he wanted to get in his car. I said Rozzie and I would get off at the lobby and he could join us in the Blue Lagoon. 'We'll all go to the basement,' Zachary said, and produced a revolver. Your man Sullivan, brave guy, made a move and was shot right between the eyes. Then I knew, much too late, what was happening.''

"You weren't armed, Major?'' Hardy said.

Willis glanced at Rozzie. "I was just taking my wife out on a date, not planning to leave the hotel. I felt perfectly safe here in the Beaumont.''

"I wish you had been,'' Chambrun said.

"No way you could possibly have foreseen it, Pierre,'' Willis said. "Anyway, I was forced, at gunpoint, to carry Sullivan's body to that trash bin. I was ordered to strip myself of my uniform and leave it there. Zachary was wearing a raincoat, and he gave it to me to put on over my shirt and underthings. We just walked out onto the street that way, walked past some backyards and into the basement of that brownstone where you found us.''

"You were badly treated, Mrs. Willis?'' Colonel Martin asked.

"Mostly just humiliated,'' Rozzie Willis said. "Fondled, pinched, handled by a big red-haired goon who was our jailer.''

"And threatened with the works if I didn't talk,'' Willis said.

"The brooch?'' Hardy asked.

"They must have known what it was for,'' Willis said. "It was ripped off Rozzie the minute we were in the basement.''

"And left in 17E to make us think you'd been brought back to the hotel,'' Hardy said.

"They told me they were going to bring Guy to where we were, and when they got through working him over in front of me, I would talk.''

"But you wouldn't, would you, Dad?" the boy asked.

The Major looked at his son. "I like to think I wouldn't, Guy," he said. "It would have been pretty rough."

"I would have come, but Mr. Chambrun wouldn't let them have me," the boy said.

"Bless you, Pierre," Willis said.

"I thought it was the only way to keep you alive till we could find you," Chambrun said.

Hardy turned to Betsy. "Did you know, Betsy, that Zachary recorded his scene with you in his apartment?"

Betsy nodded. "He played it for me later. I didn't think Pierre would be buffaloed by it—I hoped he wouldn't. Zachary rang the front doorbell at my building about four in the morning. Just after I'd left Mark here with Guy and gone home to get some sleep. He didn't bluff, said he was Captain Zachary. He couldn't locate Pierre and needed some information about hotel routines."

"This over the front-door intercom?" Hardy asked.

"Yes. So I told him to come up, let him into my place, and found out I'd been had. He went through that routine of a sexual attack—of course, I didn't know he was recording it—and when I started to scream at him he slugged me with something and I blacked out. When I came to I was being carried into the basement of that brownstone by Rozzie's 'red-haired goon.'"

"It's interesting the role that tapes play in this," Chambrun said. "Zachary used a tape to try to bluff me into turning young Guy loose, and I used a tape to nail him."

"Would you mind explaining that, Mr. Chambrun?" Colonel Martin asked.

"Half my life is spent on the telephone," Chambrun said. "I have a recorder on my desk so that I can tape any phone calls I want for later use. I also have one in the little rest room off my office. In the afternoon, while I was resting, Mrs. Veach put through a call to me from Betsy's abductor. I turned on my recorder and I tried to stall him while Mrs. Veach tried to trace the call. I knew the caller was faking his speaking voice. Eventually I told him to use his 'phony Russian accent' so I'd know I was talking to the right person. He just laughed and hung up. But that laugh did him in!"

"Explanation?" Hardy asked.

"The voice was not familiar. But that laugh! Zachary and I had not gotten along, you know. I didn't like him. I particularly didn't like him when he laughed at some suggestion I made. I don't forget the sound of someone laughing at me. That laugh, when the man hung up, was Zachary's. I played the tape over several times. No doubt of it. But would it sell anybody else? Probably not. Was it evidence that could be used in court? No way. But I knew, whether I could convince anyone else or not, who my man was."

"So you decided to play The Lone Ranger?" Hardy said, sounding just a little angry.

"Not quite," Chambrun said. "I knew if I told you there'd be cops following Zachary and he'd spot them. I knew if I told you, Colonel Martin, you'd probably think I was balmy, tell Zachary, and he'd be watching for me. I was afraid if I told you, Mark, or Jerry, that somehow even with the best intentions, you'd tip my hand. You see, knowing it was Zachary, I was convinced the hostages were being held somewhere close by, not in Cuba or Canada or someplace far away. He had to show here and he had to be able to get to them quickly if he got the boy free. So, Mike was the person I trusted because he had something I could use, an army of street kids whom Zachary would have no reason to suspect."

"They spotted Zachary and the brownstone for you?" Hardy asked.

"A couple of them spotted him coming out of the brownstone and heading for the hotel," Chambrun said.

"They knew him by sight?" Colonel Martin asked.

"He'd been pointed out to them by Mike. They reported to me. I had to decide whether to go to the house and, you might say, attack, hopeful of freeing you people. But if I went there when he wasn't there I'd never nail him. So we waited. He showed back here, and then, after a while, he headed back to the brownstone. There were kids everywhere, but invisible as far as Zachary was concerned. Why should kids be interested in him? Zachary started back. I was already stationed across the street. Suddenly, out of nowhere, there was Mark! You started across the street to him, Mark, and forgive me, but I hated you for a moment. You were going to blow it!"

"I hadn't the faintest notion that he—"

"I know," Chambrun said. "Fortunately you kept Zachary and his red-haired friend so busy that Mike's young lock-picking genius was able to get the front door open for us. The rest you all know.''

Major Hamilton Willis spoke in a slightly unsteady voice. "Once you owed me, Pierre. Now I owe you ten times over.''

''So, you're all in one piece and my hotel can start to function again. No debts, Major, just friends.'' Chambrun glanced down at the boy, sitting with his mother on the couch. "Now you can put a face to that second man in your nightmare, Guy. But you won't have to have nightmares anymore, will you?''

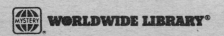